3 Days Left To Die

Mushaf Naveed

Published by Mushaf, 2024.

This is a work of fiction. Similarities to real people, places, or events are entirely coincidental.

3 DAYS LEFT TO DIE

First edition. November 23, 2024.

ISBN: 979-8230661740

Written by Mushaf Naveed.

Table of Contents

About The Author

My name is Mushaf Naveed. Because of its unusual and challenging nature, only a few people can pronounce my name correctly. Most people, however, call me whatever rolls off their tongue. I'm studying Software Engineering at Sir Syed CASE Institute and am also a writer. I'm not quite sure when I transitioned from an engineer to a writer, but I've always had a desire to hear stories and for people to hear mine. However, the kind of stories I have often invite ridicule, so I decided to write them down, realizing that readers understand much more than listeners. And besides, once words and emotions are spoken, they lose some of their value; writing them down makes them immortal for years to come.

Saying more about myself wouldn't be right. I'd prefer for people to find me within the characters I create.

Dedication

I dedicate this book to a few people who have shaped my journey. First, to my younger sister, Maliha Naveed, whose library of books and constant habit of reading sparked my own curiosity to read and write. She is truly the best. To my university friends, Manahil Khan and Moazzam Haider, whose words have always deeply touched me. To my childhood school friend, Muhammad Ali Abbasi, whose encouragement and motivation made me believe I could achieve something meaningful. And lastly, to my Dear parents, who's upbringing always made me think critically, set me apart from my peers, and gave me the chance to explore my own potential. To each of you, I am deeply grateful.

Chapter 1: A Dream

In a grand, sprawling house in Bahria Enclave, Islamabad, the morning air is thick with silence, broken only by the faint ticking of an ornate wall clock. The residence is a masterpiece of modern design—a blend of elegance and mystery. Expansive glass windows stretch from floor to ceiling, framing a panoramic view of manicured gardens and distant hills. The sleek, minimalist decor—dark marble floors, deep gray walls, and low-hanging lights casting an ambient glow—creates an atmosphere that's both luxurious and enigmatic. Every corner speaks of wealth and power, yet the shadows seem to hint at hidden secrets.

At precisely five in the morning, the sharp, insistent sound of an alarm cuts through the silence. Zarrar stirs, a frown creasing his forehead as he sits up abruptly, taking deep, measured breaths. "When will this nightmare finally release me? What do they want from me?" he mutters to himself, his voice barely a whisper as he tries to shake off the lingering dread. He's had these dreams since he was twelve—vivid, haunting visions that disturb his sleep, unsettling in their accuracy. They began as mere dreams, but over the years, Zarrar noticed a disturbing pattern: these visions would eventually unfold in reality, forcing him to question his own mind. He had never spoken about them to anyone, keeping the strange gift—or curse—hidden even from his closest family.

Today, the dream is of a catastrophic accident on Chak Shehzad Road: a brutal collision between two vehicles, so devastating that neither the cars nor the families inside remain recognizable. The horror of it weighs on him, yet, over time, he's learned to bury these thoughts deep within. He rises from the bed, pushing the nightmare aside, and begins his meticulously planned morning.

After a quick shot of espresso, Zarrar steps into his private gym, where the walls are lined with mirrors and top-of-the-line equipment gleams under the low lights. His workout regimen is strict and intense, honed over years to perfection. He starts with his warm-up—a staggering 200 push-ups, 50 pull-ups, 200 crunches, 100 squats, 50 Russian twists, and a 3-minute plank, each exercise pushing his body to the limit. The controlled rhythm of his breathing, the steady contraction and release of his muscles—all offer a kind of focus that allows him, however briefly, to forget the disturbing dreams.

His workout complete, Zarrar moves back to his room, a sanctuary of sleek furniture, dark wood, and immaculate design. A large mirror occupies one wall, reflecting his tall, well-built frame. At 28, he isn't traditionally handsome, but his chiseled physique and undeniable presence make him stand out. His dark eyes hold a quiet intensity, and his dedication to fitness has given him an air of disciplined strength.

He begins his grooming routine with almost ritualistic precision, applying creams to his face, shaving his beard meticulously to maintain a clean, sharp look, and styling his hair with careful attention. He spritzes an expensive cologne, the fragrance filling the room as he inspects his appearance in the mirror. Every detail matters to Zarrar, every step of preparation calculated to achieve perfection. For nearly an hour, he attends to his appearance, moving with an almost obsessive care, as though dressing for battle rather than a typical day at work.

Finally satisfied, Zarrar makes his way to the dining area, where Amira, his wife, is setting out breakfast with the help of their maid. She's carefully placing a plate with a fried egg, toast, and tea on the table when Zarrar's gaze lands on the plate, and his face darkens.

"Again, the same kind of egg?" His voice is sharp, a cutting tone that causes both Amira and the maid to tense. "You forget every single day that I don't like it like this—with this crispy edge around it."

Amira looks up, her voice soft but steady. "No, look... it's not like that today. I made sure it's done properly."

Zarrar's frown deepens as he studies the egg, his displeasure clear. "You think this is fine? Either you can't see or I can't," he says coldly. "I remind you every day, yet every morning, I'm met with the same disappointment."

Amira's gaze drops to the table, but she keeps her tone calm, almost placating. "I try my best. Why don't you just remove the crispy part and eat the rest?"

He scoffs, his voice growing colder. "Why don't you eat it yourself?" He turns to the maid, his words biting. "And what are you even here for if you can't manage to cook a simple egg properly?"

Amira flinches slightly, but doesn't respond, her face showing the faint strain of the exchange. Zarrar pushes back his chair abruptly, the legs scraping against the floor, startling both women. "I'm leaving. I'll have breakfast outside. You can eat this yourself," he says, his tone filled with disdain as he grabs his keys and storms out of the house.

Behind him, Amira stands silently, looking down at the plate in front of her, the tension of the morning lingering in the still air, as Zarrar's footsteps fade down the hall.

Zarrar and Amira have been married for three years, and this is the state of their marriage. To the world, they appear as husband and wife, but their conversations are limited to exchanges at the dining table. They sleep in separate rooms and have spent three years of their lives like this.

Zarrar was just like his name—stern and uncompromising. In contrast, Amira was an innocent and gentle soul, with a voice as soft as her nature. She was full of virtues, and God had blessed her with beautiful features, such as her brown eyes and hair. Strands of her hair always rolled forward toward her eyes, which she would brush aside every so often. When she smiled, deep dimples appeared on both cheeks. She always wore a delicate nose pin, adding to her charm. It's said that a nose pin enhances a woman's beauty, but she was so captivating that even the nose pin seemed almost unnecessary.

Amira spent her days immersed in household chores. Reading books is her favorite pastime. Her days were occupied either with housework, Namaz and recitation of the Holy Quran, or reading a book.

Zarrar storms out of the house, his face tight with anger. Seeing him approach, the driver rushes toward the car, but Zarrar stops him with a wave of his hand, saying, "I'll drive myself today." He gets into the car and drives off quickly. A few minutes later, he pulls out his phone and makes a call.

Zarrar: Hi! Have you reached the office already?

Sawera: Yes, zarrar, I got here bright and early.

Zarrar smiles as he replies, "Then you must be free, right?"

Sawera, laughing playfully, responds, "Just a bit of work, but why? What's the plan?"

Zarrar chuckles and says, "Forget the work. Get ready—I'll be there soon. Let's go have breakfast together."

Sawera, with a teasing tone, replies, "wait, wait. Who's going to handle all this work—are you planning to take care of it?"

Zarrar insists, "I said leave the work. Just be ready. I'll call when I arrive, and you come outside."

Sawera, laughing shyly, says, "As you wish, boss!"

Zarrar: Good. See you in a bit.*

Sawera works in Zarrar's office as an assistant to his personal secretary and has been in this role for the past five years. Though not conventionally beautiful like Amira, Sawera possesses a magnetic allure that she expertly wields to draw attention from Zarrar. She is acutely aware of her own flaws yet remains indifferent to the moral implications of her actions. She thrives on the validation she receives from Zarrar, understanding the dynamics of their relationship, but simultaneously maintains a connection with another man for added affirmation. She knows she is crossing boundaries but feels entitled to do so, believing that her needs and desires take precedence. Sawera's dark hair, black eyes and sharp features give her an edgy presence, and her keen intellect enables her to navigate the complexities of office politics, further entrenching her position in Zarrar's life. **If there is anyone in this entire world who is the most important to Zarrar, it is Sawera.**

Zarrar and Sawra are having breakfast at a beautiful restaurant, Chai Khana, located in I8. The soft morning light is casting a warm glow over their table, adorned with a delightful array of breakfast items. Golden fried eggs, aromatic tea, and pancakes are artfully arranged, creating a vibrant scene. Zarrar's face carries a deep furrow of contemplation, as if burdened by an invisible weight.

After finishing breakfast, Zarrar lights up a cigarette, swirling the smoke into intricate rings as he initiates a conversation.

Zarrar (with worry and frustration): Life has become a torment for me. There isn't a single day when I feel at peace. The trouble my uncle left on my shoulders is something I can't escape, no matter how hard I try. I'm fed up with it; nothing she does seems right to me. It drives me crazy. I'm just so tired of it all.

Sawera (smiling): Oh, so that's why our Zarrar is sad today.

Zarrar: I'm not sad; it doesn't affect me.

Sawera (in a loving tone): Look, Zarrar, I don't know what you think of me, but you know I never say anything wrong. But why can't you just let her go? Free that innocent girl; she's beautiful, and someone else will come along for her too. Look, I'm saying this again because I'm telling you the truth—what you're doing is wrong for both yourself and her.

Zarrar (raising his voice slightly): Me? What am I doing wrong?

Sawera (explaining): You're not giving her the happiness she deserves. She wants to feel joy too; she wants to envision a bright future with someone. What is she getting from you? Pain—just pain. Let her go and allow her to live her life as she wishes. You're doing wrong to yourself too. Don't you deserve to be happy? Every person, every man wants to be happy. When he comes home, he wants his exhaustion to fade away. But look at yourself. Take care of yourself, Zarrar; I can't stand seeing you like this. If you're not happy, it doesn't matter how wealthy you are.

Zarrar (innocently and helplessly): I can't let her go; I wish I could.

Sawera (with a hint of bitterness): Why can't you? **Just marry me**. I'll take care of you. Look, try to understand my point; you're happy with me. I'm with you in joy and sorrow. Don't you think those who are happy together should have the right to live their lives together? Lighten Amira's burden by freeing her and lighten your own load so you can be happy. I will be with you; we've been together for a long time. What else does a person need in this world if love is in front of them and it's easy to attain?

Zarrar (smiling): No, it's not like that; it's not that simple. I like you; you know that well, but give me some time to think. You're absolutely right, but I need some time.

Sawera (smirking): That's what you always say, Zarrar; this is nothing new.

Zarrar (holding her hand): Sawera, just drop all this; it's our never-ending debate. You were supposed to go shopping, right? Let's go now.

Sawera (changing her expression): No, I'm not going anywhere. I'm just going to the office.

Zarrar (laughing): But I'm going shopping, and you will come with me.

Sawera (laughing): Zarrar, why do you tease me every day?

Zarrar smiles as he replies, "Because I enjoy it—and you're the only one I tease. Aren't you going to start making Snaps and Insta Stories once we're there?"

Sawera laughs and says, "Oh, I'll do that with pleasure!"

Zarrar: "I don't like Snapchat at all."

Sawera: "Well, that's just how I am—love me as I am if you truly care, Zarrar."

Zarrar: "Alright! But shall we go now, madam?"

Sawera laughs and says, "Yes, sir, let's go."

After a long shopping trip, Sawera arrives back at the office. Her shopping bags are still in Zarrar's car as he heads to his room. On her way to her own office, she hears Adeel's voice from behind.

"Had a nice breakfast, madam?" Adeel says in a light, sarcastic tone. Sawera turns around, giving him a soft smile as she responds, "Adeel, why do you always make comments like this?"

With a slight grin, Adeel replies, "What kind of comments do I make?"

Sawera looks at him knowingly and says, "You're overthinking things again, Adeel..."

Adeel chuckles in a sarcastic tone, "Yes, of course, I'm always the one overthinking, right? When was I ever right about anything?"

Noticing the disappointment in his eyes, Sawera pauses and asks gently, "Shall we go inside and talk?"

Adeel, smiling earnestly, responds, "It would be my pleasure, Sawera."

Sawera smiles back, and they both walk into the room together.

Adeel is a deeply loyal and hardworking employee, well-respected in the company for his dedication and kindness. His quiet, steadfast love for Sawera has anchored him through countless hours of listening to her thoughts, soothing her moods, and supporting her through every challenge. Despite his deep affection, he remains aware that, for Sawera, he is mostly a close friend, perhaps even a backup, while her heart truly belongs to Zarrar. His modest style—a neatly trimmed beard and simple, well-kept haircut—reflects his grounded nature, making him both approachable and admirable.

They both settle into the couches across from each other, an uneasy silence filling the room. Sawera sighs, glancing at Adeel. "Look, Adeel, we're just good friends. That's it. He was going through something, and I was there for him. There's nothing more to it, like you're thinking."

Adeel nods slightly, a flicker of disappointment in his eyes. "I understand, Sawera. But you do things for him you never do for me. How long has it been since we've gone out together? You're with him all the time."

Sawera's brow furrows. She responds firmly, "Adeel, you're seriously frustrating me right now. Anytime I've had an issue, you've been there, in every joy, every sorrow. You're not just a friend; you're more than that. If you weren't important to me, why would I even explain all this to you?"

Adeel, with a hint of resignation, says, "I get it, Sawera. But try to understand me too; it doesn't sit well with me. Anyway, forgive me. It won't happen again, I promise."

Sawera smirks, half-amused, half-irritated. "You shouldn't be thinking about all this anyway. You should know where you stand with me. Now, I'm mad at you. Don't talk to me. Go away, Adeel." She turns her gaze aside, feigning annoyance.

Adeel laughs, saying, "If you're upset, then I'm supposed to make it up to you. So, tonight, let's go out for dinner. Just us, alright?"

Sawera, half-heartedly, says, "Adeel, not tonight, please. I have a lot of work. Tomorrow, maybe, but not today."

Adeel, smirking, teases, "Alright, alright. I'm not Zarrar after all."

Sawera laughs, "Fine, let's go then, happy?"

Adeel stands up, grinning ear to ear. "Happy? I'm ecstatic!"

Sawera smiles, "Just stay that way, but please, let me work for a bit, will you?"

Adeel laughs, "Alright, alright, do your work. Let me know if you need anything. See you tonight."

Sawera smiles as he leaves the room, a faint warmth lingering on both their faces.

In the sleek conference room, the lights are dim, and the long, polished table gleams under the overhead lights. Outside the glass windows, the cityscape of Islamabad stretches under the morning haze, but inside, tension thickens as Zarrar flips through the presentation documents with a deepening frown.

He slams the file shut, his fingers tightening around it. "Where is Anum?" he barks, his voice echoing sharply in the large room.

Within seconds, Anum hurries in, her face a mix of concern and professionalism. Her modest, neatly ironed dress and the faint smile on her face suggest her gentle nature—a stark contrast to the man glowering at her from the head of the table.

"Sir, you called?" she asks politely, standing with her hands clasped nervously in front of her.

Zarrar doesn't even look up. "Why isn't this report finished?" He flips the file open again, his eyes narrowing on the incomplete slides. "Do you think this is acceptable? We have a client meeting in thirty minutes, and this is all you've prepared?"

Anum's eyes widen slightly, but she keeps her voice steady. "Sir, I assigned the report sections to Sawera, as per your instructions. She was to handle the final presentation. I thought—"

"Don't give me excuses!" Zarrar snaps, his tone venomous. "You're my secretary, aren't you? Sawera is just an assistant. If something's missing, the responsibility is yours."

Anum glances down, swallowing hard. "Sir, I... I did try to check in with Sawera, but she assured me everything was under control. I believed—"

"That's the problem, Anum," Zarrar interrupts coldly, his voice dripping with disdain. "You *believe* too much. This isn't some charity where we 'believe' things will magically get done. If you can't handle a simple report, then maybe you're not fit for this role."

Anum's face flushes with embarrassment. She looks down, biting her lip. "I apologize, sir. I didn't mean for it to come to this."

"Apologies don't mean anything to me, Anum." Zarrar's voice is razor-sharp, his gaze fixed on her with undisguised contempt. "The clients don't want apologies either. They want results, something you clearly don't understand."

Anum's shoulders slump slightly, yet she remains composed. "I will have it completed right away, sir," she says quietly, but her voice carries a tinge of desperation.

Zarrar scoffs, clearly unimpressed. "Oh, now you're going to finish it in a matter of minutes? Tell me, Anum, what were you doing when this needed to be done? Sitting around, sipping coffee with Sawera? Or just daydreaming while she ran circles around you?"

Anum looks up, her gentle eyes pleading. "Sir, I really did my best. Sawera assured me—"

"Sawera this, Sawera that!" Zarrar cuts her off with a wave of his hand, dismissing her words as if they're beneath him. "You're my secretary, Anum. The responsibility is on you. If Sawera wasn't competent, why did you trust her? Maybe I should find someone who knows how to do their job without clinging to excuses."

Anum's lips tremble, but she holds herself together. "I understand, sir. I will improve, and I'll make sure it's complete before the meeting," she says softly, her humility somehow making Zarrar's coldness seem even more brutal.

Zarrar leans back in his chair, a smirk of satisfaction flickering across his face. "Better," he mutters. "I need perfection, Anum, not excuses. Do you understand that?"

"Yes, sir." Her voice barely rises above a whisper, but she stands tall, refusing to let his words break her composure.

"Good. Now get out. I don't want to see you until it's done." Zarrar's words are a dismissal as he looks away, already flipping open his laptop as if she no longer exists.

Anum nods and leaves the room, her face flushed, hands trembling slightly as she walks back to her desk. The door swings shut behind her, leaving Zarrar alone with his thoughts, entirely unfazed by the impact of his words.

Not far from the conference room, Sawera watches the scene from her desk, a smirk of satisfaction on her lips. She goes back to her work, unconcerned with the incomplete report or the responsibility Anum has now been unfairly burdened with. For her, Zarrar's favoritism is something she's come to expect—and exploit.

Back in the conference room, Zarrar leans back, his gaze fixed on the city outside, unfazed by the injustice he's just dealt to his loyal secretary. For him, Anum's devotion and humility mean little. He thrives on control, and in his world, a mere secretary's feelings and reputation are as expendable as the paper in front of him.

The night was calm, and the sky glittered with stars beneath the full moon's glow, creating a peaceful atmosphere. Yet, paradoxically, within this serene setting lingered the shadows of troubled souls. Zarrar, having left his office, was driving home in his Toyota Vigo Champ GX, enjoying the music and lost in his thoughts. Suddenly, an old beggar approached his car, hand outstretched, seeking some help. Zarrar initially ignored him, but the beggar persisted, knocking gently on his car window.

Annoyed, Zarrar rolled down the window and asked harshly, "What's your problem?"

With a voice full of desperation, the beggar replied, "Brother, please, help me a little. I'm starving."

Zarrar smirked sarcastically, lit a cigarette, and took a drag before blowing smoke right in the beggar's face. The old man flinched, waving the smoke away and staring in shock at Zarrar. In a voice filled with pain, he said, "Sir, if you don't want to help, don't. But please, don't insult me like this."

Zarrar let out a mocking laugh. "Insulting you?" he sneered. "Weren't you the same person I saw this morning on the corner of this road, smoking away? Let me tell you something—I don't earn this money to fund addicts like you, understand?"

The beggar looked at Zarrar, disappointment and helplessness etched on his face, and replied, "You're truly a rude person, sir. If you won't help, then don't, but don't humiliate me."

The beggar turned to leave, but Zarrar shouted after him, "Get lost! And don't ever come near my car again. Otherwise, next time, I'll break your bones."

Just then, the signal turned green, and Zarrar drove off quickly, retreating back into his own world as though nothing had happened. Behind him, the old beggar stood in the darkness, his wounded heart carrying the weight of another night's misery.

Zarrar drives a little further when he sees two cars collide on the adjacent road. It's exactly what he had seen in his dreams. He glances at the scene but drives past without stopping. "What foolish people," he mutters to himself. "Why do they have to interfere with my dreams? They've ruined my strange life." Anger wells up inside him as he grumbles to himself.

As Zarrar steps into the house, Amira rushes toward him, her face filled with softness, and her eyes bearing the innocence of a heartfelt apology. She greets him and, in a single breath, says, "I wanted to apologize for this morning.

It won't happen again. But I've prepared a delicious meal—pilao with beef. You'll love it." She speaks as if she had rehearsed it all in her mind.

Zarrar pauses, looking at her in silence for a few moments, a faint smile forming on his lips. He nods gently and replies, "It's fine. But I won't be able to eat. I had plenty during the day and I'm not really hungry right now. I'm sorry."

Amira's smile fades slightly, and a hint of disappointment clouds her eyes. Yet, with tender grace, she says, "That's alright. Please, go and rest."

Her voice quivers ever so slightly, but her gaze remains warm, as though Zarrar's comfort meant more to her than anything else.

It's around 9:30 at night. Zarrar lies on his bed, scrolling through his phone, when a gentle knock echoes at the door. He calls out, "Come in." Amira enters, holding a glass of water. With a soft, loving smile, she says, "I brought you some water... so you can drink it easily if you feel thirsty during the night."

Without looking up, Zarrar responds nonchalantly, "Thanks... just put it there."

Amira quietly places the glass on the table and turns to leave. As she reaches the door, she pauses, glancing back, hoping he might acknowledge her, show some sign of warmth. But Zarrar remains absorbed in his phone, oblivious to her presence.

She lets out a silent sigh, closes the door gently behind her, and leaves the room.

Zarrar continues on his phone for a while longer, then eventually lays back and falls asleep, as if nothing had happened.

The day appeared as dark as night, as if shrouded in shadow. Amid the storm's roar, a man stood on the road, dressed impeccably in a black suit, clutching a bouquet of flowers. Rain fell heavily, drenching him completely, while thunder echoed in the distance. He held a phone to his ear, and through the speaker came a strange, crackling voice, hauntingly repeating, "Zarrar, where are you? Zarrar, where are you?" The question echoed, lost yet insistent, as though calling him from somewhere far away. The man's gaze dropped to his wristwatch, which showed 5:00 PM, October 23, 2024.

Just then, headlights pierced through the storm, speeding towards him down the rain-slicked road. The car hurtled closer, splashing water in its wake, appearing more menacing with every second. Yet the man didn't move. His eyes remained fixed ahead, as if he had neither the will nor intention to escape. In mere moments, the car struck him with a brutal force, flinging his body onto the drenched road. Blood began to trickle down his face, merging with the relentless rain, his eyes staring blankly ahead.

He lay motionless on the ground, rain pouring down around him, when another figure—a stranger—paused and knelt beside him, gently lifting his broken body from the road. In the storm's eerie light, the stranger's face became visible. And in a chilling moment of realization, Zarrar, within his dream, saw himself staring at his own lifeless face. **That bloodied, unseeing face was none other than his own.** Thunder crashed loudly, and Zarrar awoke with a scream, jolted from the nightmare.

Chapter 2: BETWEEN CHAOS AND SILENCE

October 21, 2024

Zarrar jolts awake, drenched in sweat, his room filled with an eerie silence, save for the relentless beeping of his alarm. "Will I die in three days?" This question seems to echo from all around him. His body shivers with fear, and he keeps muttering, "Will I die in three days?"

His eyes dart nervously around the room, from one corner to the other. Sometimes, he anxiously runs his hand through his hair, at other times, he tries to reassure himself, "No, nothing is going to happen. It's just a dream." He is so deeply lost in these thoughts that he doesn't even notice the alarm continuing to ring. The sound becomes so loud that Amira rushes in from the next room. In surprise, she opens the door and asks, "Are you okay?"

Zarrar, still dazed, stares at her without answering. When she gets no response, Amira steps closer and asks, "Zarrar, are you alright? Did something happen? Did you have a nightmare?" Her words bring him back to his senses. He replies, "What? No, no, nothing's wrong. Why would anything be wrong?" He smiles, but his voice quivers, and fear lingers in his eyes.

"Are you really okay?" Amira asks once more.

"Yes, I'm fine... but why are you here?" Zarrar asks.

"Your alarm was ringing, and you didn't turn it off, so I got worried. You never do that," Amira answers cautiously.

"No, I'm fine. Go back to your room. Nothing's wrong," Zarrar insists.

Amira leaves, though she knows something is wrong with him. His pale face gave away that something had happened, though she thought it was just a bad dream. But it wasn't just a nightmare...

Zarrar sits on the edge of his bed, his mind racing, trying to understand what just happened. He refuses to believe it was merely a dream. Lost in confusion and anxiety, he watches the sunrise as birds begin their morning songs. A soft ray of sunlight starts to brighten his room. He gets up,walks to the window, and pulls aside the curtain. The gentle morning light touches his face as he gazes outside, fixated on a tree, lost in thought.

Today, Zarrar doesn't work out. He just sits quietly in his room. When it's time for breakfast, he gets up and goes to the table, where Amira brings him his meal. The fried egg is exactly how he likes it today, but Zarrar eats in silence, without saying a word. The sadness on his face is clearly visible.

After breakfast, he leaves the house for work, dressed in a black two-piece suit, but without a tie. The weight of his thoughts and the unease from the morning still lingers as he steps out the door. Zarrar is driving, but his mind is lost in a whirlwind of thoughts. He feels restless, with worry and fear clearly visible on his face. He still can't believe that he only has three days left to live. Muttering to himself, he repeats, "I can't die, why would I die? It doesn't happen like this. I won't die."

In this anxious state, he continues driving, when suddenly, a car overtakes him at high speed. His own car, now out of control due to the sudden jolt, swerves wildly from side to side. With great difficulty, Zarrar manages to regain control, narrowly avoiding crashing into the sidewalk. With a sharp pull, he brings the car to a halt.

As the car comes to a stop, Zarrar exhales a long, relieved breath, his heart still racing from the near accident. It had become clear to Zarrar that he was no longer in control of his senses. He knew he couldn't focus on work, so he pulled out his phone and called Savera.

Zarrar: "Hello... I won't be coming to the office today. You handle things."

Savera: "Why aren't you coming? Everything alright, Zarrar?"

Zarrar: "Yes, everything's fine. I'm just not in the mood."

Savera, in a playful tone, responded, "Wow! Look at that—our boss is in a mood today!"

Zarrar chuckled and then hung up the phone.

He didn't know what to do next, so he turned off the car and stepped out onto the road. He began walking aimlessly, his mind racing with endless questions. Lost in his thoughts, he just kept walking, unaware of where he was going or why. His mind was a mess. "Why do I keep having these dreams? Why only me? I wish these dreams would stop." Sometimes he thought, "I've worked so hard my whole life. I can't die this soon. It can't happen to me." Other times, he pondered, "What if it's all a lie? Not all my dreams have come true; many of them never happened."

Passersby glanced at him curiously as he wandered, talking to himself, wondering if he was mad. "Is this guy crazy? He doesn't look like it."

This was the same Zarrar who couldn't stand heat for a moment and had air conditioning installed from his car to his home and office doors. Yet today, he had been walking in the scorching sun on Park Road for the past hour and a half, completely unaware of why or where he was going. He had walked from Bani Gala all the way to COMSATS(4-5km) University without even realizing the distance he had covered.

Such is human nature—when everything is available, gratitude fades away. We forget that life's blessings are gifts, capable of being taken away just as easily. The hunger for more never ends. Even if humans were given the moon, they would still find faults in it. Perhaps this is why mankind has never repaid the debt to the Earth, the very ground on which we walk.

We don't recognize how peace and comfort can lead to destruction. When all our worries disappear, we find new ones, sometimes imaginary ones. This is why nations blessed with peace are often the ones where humanity, relationships, and emotions are dying. Thousands of years ago, humans fought for their land and worked tirelessly to survive. There was no time for depression or anxiety; they were constantly creating, and building. But now, when people lie in comfort, they obsess over trivial things that didn't even exist before.

For the first time in history, there are more than two genders, war-torn countries lack bread to eat, while in wealthy nations, a person looks at a burger and feels anxious. Someone in a war-torn country may have lost everything and still manage to smile, while someone with everything in the world is found hanging from a ceiling fan.

Peace and comfort are only pleasant within limits. When life becomes devoid of struggle, people start tearing at their flesh.

As he continued walking, he found himself on a road lined with tall trees on both sides. It was a long and pristine road, almost like a hidden path to a secret paradise. Anyone who traveled down this road knew that even the slightest breeze would enhance its beauty to such an extent that it was impossible not to pull over, step out, and take in the breathtaking scenery. This was a single-lane road, and every year in October, dry, crimson leaves would be scattered across it, adding even more charm to its allure. It felt as though the road itself had embraced the earth in a tranquil repose. Yet, strangely enough, only a few people knew about this road, and even among those who passed through, only a handful could truly appreciate its beauty.

Zarrar is captivated by the beauty of the road. He stops to take in the view and then begins to walk along it.A man, perhaps in his early thirties, appeared from nowhere, skipping and hopping his way over, drawing curious looks with his erratic movements. His *shalwar kameez* (a popular outfit in Pakistan, Bangladesh, and India) hung loosely, the buttons undone, giving him an untamed appearance. Children watched as he danced, twirled, and played games on an invisible board on the ground. Lost in his world, he suddenly spotted Zarrar, who was lost in his thoughts. The man burst forward, stopping just inches from Zarrar's face, his eyes wide with excitement, as he declared in a wavering, thrilled voice, **"Shani! It's going to be great! Shani's going to have fun! Mom's making parathas; it's going to be amazing! Shani's happy, Shani's so happy!"**

Zarrar, taken aback by the intensity of this stranger, narrowed his eyes, visibly disturbed. **"You're a madman. Get away from me,"** he muttered, sidestepping him, leaving the man—Shani—oblivious to Zarrar's annoyance as he bounced off, still lost in his world. After some time, when fatigue sets in, he sits down on a bench. It's a beautiful October day, with a cool breeze blowing, and red, dried leaves scattered around the bench, dancing in the wind. As Zarrar observes this picturesque scene, he notices an elderly man sitting on a nearby bench. The old man has been sitting there for quite some time, quietly gazing at the forest ahead. Zarrar watches him, puzzled by the sight. His curiosity grows as he wonders why the old man has been staring at the forest for so long, sitting motionless in the same spot. Intrigued, Zarrar feels an urge to approach the elderly man and ask what has kept him so engrossed in this silent observation.

Zarrar shifts slightly on the bench and, facing the elderly man, greets him loudly with a "Salaam." The old man remains absorbed in his own world, not responding. Noticing the lack of reply, Zarrar calls out again, even louder this time. The elderly man turns, as though reluctantly stirred from a deep slumber. He responds to the greeting with warmth, as if he recognizes Zarrar, and then immediately turns back to gaze at the forest ahead. Zarrar is puzzled by the man's silence and his unwavering attention toward the forest. Now, feeling more curious, Zarrar moves a bit closer and softly asks, "If you don't mind, may I ask you something?" The elderly man turns again, this time smiling kindly, and replies, "Yes, of course, my boy. Go ahead, ask." Zarrar hesitates, carefully choosing his words, and then speaks, "I've been watching you for quite a while now. You've been sitting here, just staring at the forest." He pauses, trying to phrase his question more clearly. "I mean, it seems like you've been looking at nothing but the forest for a long time. Why? What's in that forest?" The elderly man listens patiently to Zarrar's question, and after a moment, he begins to laugh. Zarrar, surprised by the laughter, wonders what is so amusing. The man finally stops laughing and says, **"My boy, In the silence of the forest, there's more noise than in the chaos of the city."** With that, the elderly man returns to his quiet contemplation, leaving Zarrar intrigued and bewildered. The cryptic response stirs something within him, filling him with curiosity. He begins to ponder the old man's words, wondering what deeper meaning they might hold. After a moment of contemplation, Zarrar turns back to the man and asks, "I didn't quite understand what you meant. What are you trying to say?"

The elderly man appears to be in his mid-70s to 80s. He has striking blue eyes and a short beard. Despite his age, he seems to be in good health, though his deep voice carries a slight tremor. Speaking at length causes him to become short of breath, making it difficult for him to engage in long conversations. The elderly man is dressed in a traditional white *shalwar kameez* (a popular outfit in Pakistan, Bangladesh, and India), with a gray sweater layered on top. He grips a black cane in his hand, which he relies on for support as he walks. His appearance, along with the cane, gives him a dignified presence, though it's clear the cane is essential for his movement.

The elder man turns and smiles as he responds, "Son, we are so consumed by our daily lives, burdened by endless worries, running in a race we neither understand nor know the end of. Everyone is running, some deceiving others, while some weep for someone. Somewhere, love is being showered, and somewhere else, hatred is brewing in someone's heart. Everyone is fixated on money—working tirelessly like slaves just to gather more. The more money they collect, the more their hunger grows. Every person is trying to outdo the other. They place food in front of them, but before they eat, they take a picture to show the world, only then do they start eating. We've confined ourselves to our rooms, adopting other people's personalities. This is the city—look how noisy it is. There's chaos everywhere, restlessness, and unease."

The elder coughs between every few sentences, pauses, and then softly continues, "Now, look in front of you. This is the forest. There's silence here, but do you know that someone lives here too? A whole world exists here—a realm that thrives in this very stillness, but its noise is not audible to you. This forest is like your heart, like mine. There's another world inside of us that we never experience, because we're so lost in the gatherings of this outer world that we never realize the world that exists within us. What do I want? Where do I find peace? What are my true desires? All these questions are born within us and often die within us."

The elder coughs again. Zarrar listens to his words with such fascination, like a child seeing something for the first time. The elder continues, "You must have seen people like me, elderly folks, sitting alone at this age. Sometimes, staring at the sky, sometimes at a ceiling fan, sometimes at the people around us. We too spent our lives running, just like you, but it's only at this stage, when we sat with ourselves, that we realized we wasted our lives. Where's all the money I worked so hard to earn? I'm a heart patient, and the doctor has told me I only have my medications to rely on. But I also know that one night, I might just pass away in my sleep. The home I built with my sweat and labor—the same house—my children don't let me live beyond a single room. The very children I starved myself for, to feed them, now barely come when I call them. That's why you've seen people like me sitting silently, talking to themselves, reflecting. At this age, we realize that we wasted our lives. You've probably also seen people who, after fighting all their lives, finally forgive each other in old age, because they realize there was nothing to gain from those fights. It was all so meaningless—childish even. It's only at this stage that a person understands when death feels close and life's end is near, that they wish for another chance to live again. But time has already run out. **This is life—when you realize its beauty and importance, that's when your breaths are numbered.**"

The elder coughs again and falls silent, gazing at the forest ahead. His words deeply affect Zarrar, and he too begins to stare at the forest, as questions start swirling in his mind, leaving him completely lost in thought.

A long silence falls between them. Both the elder and Zarrar sit on the bench, staring at the forest ahead. The quiet stretches on until, finally, Zarrar breaks it and asks, "Your children, do they not live with you?"

The elder, with a deep sadness in his eyes, turns to him and replies, "I try to live with them, otherwise, they wouldn't keep me."

The elder then begins to tell Zarrar his story.

The elder had served in government service for over 40 years. His wife had passed away when she was just 30 years old, leaving him with two sons. He raised both of his boys on his own, working hard to provide for them and ensure they grew up well. However, the reality he now faced was stark and heartbreaking—neither of his sons was willing to keep him permanently in their home. He was shuffled between them, living with one for a while and then the other. Often, he would only get to eat once a day, as there was no one to offer him more meals. Because of this neglect, the elder had begun to spend less and less time at home. Each morning, he would wake up for Fajr prayers and come to the park, staying there until after Zuhr, when he would finally return. He had a heart condition, and every Eid, his children would argue, not over celebrating together, but over who would have to take their father in, or how to divide his property after his passing.

After sharing his story, the elder sighed and continued, "Son, that's just how this world works. Your value here only lasts as long as you're providing something to others. Parents had respect while they were feeding their children, but once it's the children's turn to give, that respect vanishes. The very parents who raised their kids end up becoming burdens. This is how the world operates. If you're offering something beneficial, you're irreplaceable. But the moment you become a burden, you lose your worth."

He chuckled softly before continuing, "Listen, son, remember one thing in life: if you ask someone why they love you, and they can give you a reason, then know that their love isn't real. They love those reasons, not you." Seeing the confusion on Zarrar's face, the elder smiled warmly. "I understand, it seems you didn't quite grasp it. Let me explain. If someone loves you because of certain qualities—your voice, your eyes, your appearance—there may come a time when those qualities fade. As a person ages, beauty changes, it diminishes. But if someone loves you without knowing why, that is real love. Think about how your parents love you, no matter what you do, how you look, you will always be their moon."

The elder paused, watching Zarrar closely, and added, "So, remember this: **real love doesn't have a reason**. If you're doing things just to please others, they'll stay happy with you only as long as you're giving them reasons. Once those reasons fade, people change, and you'll become a burden to them. There's only one beautiful way to live in this world, and that's through love—love without conditions or reasons. Fill your daily life with this kind of love, and everything will become easier. Do your work not because you have to, but because you love it. That way, not only will the tasks become easier, but you'll find peace in doing them. If there's anything that can save this world, it's love."

Zarrar listened intently, now quiet, as he stared at the forest before them. Slowly, the elder's words began to make sense to him. He drifted into his thoughts, lost in contemplation.

Chapter 3: The Confession of Silence

In the soft, cool winds of October, dry red leaves continued to fall, covering the road beneath them. Zarrar occasionally glanced at the passing people, then shifted his gaze towards the forest, as if lost in his own thoughts. Amidst this, the sound of the call to prayer for Zuhr echoed from the mosque. The old man looked at Zarrar and said, "Come on, let's go for the prayer."

Zarrar's forehead creased with worry upon hearing this. After a brief silence, he responded, "You go ahead, I'll be there soon."

In truth, Zarrar had long since become disillusioned with the concept of God. He had abandoned his faith, believing that God held no real meaning in his life. To him, if God truly existed and loved His creations more than seventy mothers, as people claimed, why then did He inflict hardships on humanity? Why did He not come to their aid? Why did He leave people to face their struggles alone? Such questions had taken root in his mind, and when no satisfactory answers came, he had chosen to reject the very existence of God.

He gets up and starts walking toward the mosque. As he walks, his mind is flooded with thoughts. He realizes how long it has been since he last prayed, and now he can't even remember how many units (rak'ahs) there are or what exactly needs to be done during prayer. Standing at the steps of the mosque, he's lost in thought, unsure whether to go inside or not. Just then, a voice from behind interrupts him, "Move ahead, please, so others can enter too." Slowly, Zarrar steps inside the mosque.

He looks around in awe at the beauty of the mosque. His eyes wander from corner to corner, taking in the calm and serene atmosphere. Then his gaze lands on the ablution area, and it hits him—he needs to perform ablution (wudu) before he can pray. But as he walks toward the ablution area, he suddenly realizes that he doesn't remember how to do it properly anymore. He watches a man nearby as he begins to make wudu. Quietly, Zarrar sits down and starts copying the man's movements, step by step, hoping not to make any mistakes. As he completes the wudu, a wave of relief washes over him. He's pleased that he managed to do it without embarrassing himself in front of others. Zarrar then heads to the prayer row and sits down, looking around at the other worshippers who are already focused on their prayers. He observes them intently, deep in thought. Everything around him feels both familiar and foreign at the same time—like he's trying to remember something he once knew but had forgotten.

As Zarrar sits in the mosque, the tranquil atmosphere seems to amplify the silence within him, and his thoughts begin to wander back to a memory he had long tried to forget. The peacefulness around him stirs a deep, painful recollection—one he had buried for years but now rises to the surface like an unresolved shadow.

He thinks of Ali.

Ali had been more than just a friend; he had been a brother in spirit, a man of unwavering loyalty, modesty, and deep faith. Ali was the kind of person whose integrity shone through in every aspect of his life—humble, religious, and always guided by the principles of honesty and trustworthiness. In their early days of business, Ali had stood by Zarrar's side, offering his support and friendship with no hidden motives.

But Zarrar had betrayed that trust. In the early days, driven by greed, ambition, and the ruthless desire to succeed, Zarrar had orchestrated a deal that deceived Ali. It was a business transaction with the promise of great profit, and Zarrar, in his desperation, had manipulated the situation to benefit only himself. Ali had been left with nothing. Zarrar remembers that day with a growing sense of shame. He had justified it to himself at the time, convincing himself that business was brutal and survival meant stepping over others—even if that "other" was his closest friend. He had told himself Ali would understand or that he was too naive to compete in the harsh world of business. But deep down, Zarrar had known the truth: Ali didn't lose because he was weak or naive—he lost because Zarrar had wronged him. Ali's reaction still haunts Zarrar. He didn't shout, didn't curse, didn't even confront Zarrar with anger. Instead, Ali had simply walked away—his faith in their friendship shattered, his heart quietly broken. That look in Ali's eyes—the silent betrayal, the hurt, the disbelief—comes rushing back to Zarrar now, cutting him to the core. Ali had lost more than money that day; he had lost his faith in a person he thought would never harm him. Despite everything, Ali had carried himself with dignity, perhaps placing his faith in God to seek justice where Zarrar had failed him. Sitting in the mosque, Zarrar feels an overwhelming wave of guilt crash over him. He had betrayed not just a friend but a man of profound faith and integrity. The success he gained from that deal had never filled the void left by Ali's absence in his life. Zarrar realizes now, more than ever, that no amount of profit had been worth the loss of such a pure, unshakeable friendship. As the call to prayer echoes through the mosque, Zarrar's heart tightens with remorse. He had taken advantage of a man who embodied the values Zarrar had once dismissed as weakness. The years had passed, but the weight of his betrayal had stayed with him. In the silence of the mosque, he confronts the truth: Ali's trust had been priceless, and Zarrar had carelessly thrown it away.

With the prayers about to begin, Zarrar sits quietly, overwhelmed by the realization of his wrongdoing. He wonders if Ali had ever forgiven him, if there was any chance to make amends. But more than that, he wonders if he could ever forgive himself. As the first takbir is called, Zarrar feels the weight of his past pressing down on him. This time, as he prepares to stand before God, he feels the true burden of his sins—especially the one that had cost him his dearest friend, Ali.

Zarrar begins the prayer behind the Imam and realizes that he hasn't forgotten how to pray after all. He feels a wave of happiness as the verses flow from his tongue effortlessly. As he continues praying, a strange sense of peace washes over him. He completes the entire prayer and is surprised at the calmness he feels, almost as if he has discovered something new within himself.

He notices that people are leaving after the prayer, but the Imam is still in the mosque. Zarrar gets up and walks over to sit beside him. The Imam, noticing him, greets him with peace. Sensing that the young man has something on his mind, the Imam gives him a warm smile.

Zarrar returns the greeting and, with great affection, says, "Sir! Can I ask you something?"

The Imam replies, "Yes, of course! Ask away. I will do my best to give you a good answer."

Zarrar: "I've faced many hardships in my life. People say that God loves His servants more than seventy mothers. Then why did God put me through so many difficulties? Would any mother treat her child this way?"

Imam: "Hardships, my son, are not signs of God's anger or His absence. They are a test of your patience, your strength, and your faith. Just as the finest steel is forged in the hottest fire, so too are strong souls refined through trials. God doesn't give us challenges to break us, but to make us stronger and bring us closer to Him. A mother's love is boundless, but even she knows that sometimes her child must face the difficulties of life in order to grow and learn. Similarly, God tests His beloved servants because within these trials lie wisdom, strength, and, ultimately, peace.

"Remember, it is always the king in the palace who becomes corrupt and ruins his kingdom, while it is the young man on the horse who builds the empire. **Success is one of the heaviest burdens in the world,** and it is hard for anyone to handle, even for oneself. Only those who have faced difficult times truly understand how to carry success. God puts His dearest servants through hardships to see if they are worthy of the responsibilities He plans to give them. So, if you're facing difficult times, know that it's likely for your own betterment."

The Imam's words echoed in Zarrar's heart, forcing him to reconsider his old doubts. Perhaps now he was beginning to understand that his difficulties were not punishments but part of a greater, unseen wisdom. Zarrar realized that the Imam wasn't passing any judgment or issuing a fatwa but was instead guiding him toward self-reflection and improvement.

Encouraged by the Imam's calm and thoughtful approach, Zarrar posed another question: "How will I know that God exists? How will I know that if He does, He wants good for me? And if God exists, why can't I see Him?"

These three questions could easily anger someone, but a wise person listens patiently, no matter how difficult or unsettling the question may be.

Imam:

"I will answer your first question... 'How will I know that God exists?'

When you have everything and still feel restless, you will know that God exists.

When you are without a clear destination, you will realize that God exists.

When you see your efforts crumbling, it is then that you will feel the presence of God.

In the changing seasons, in the raindrops, in the fury of storms,
In your helplessness, in your desires,
In the habits that form suddenly, in those that never fade,
In the shifting colors of the sky,
In the love you give boundlessly to someone, yet they will reject you,
and in the love someone gives you unconditionally, yet you will turn them away.
In the fast passage of time, or in the moments that seem to never pass,
In your health and in your sickness,
You will see God everywhere.
In your struggles, in your joys,
In moments of solitude, or in the vastness of open fields,
In the depths of the ocean, in the peaks of mountains,
He was always with you.
You forgot Him,
Though He was closer to you than your own jugular vein,
He was the voice inside you,
When you thought of committing a sin or doing an act of goodness.
He was always with you,
But you were so absorbed in the world's distractions
That you saw everything,
But you failed to recognize the truth within your own soul.
And you ask why He does not appear to you?
If He appeared, how would your test remain?
When the teacher is not watching, that's when the student cheats,
When the beloved is not present, that's when betrayal happens.
God wanted to test you,
He wanted to see who would remain loyal to His law
Even when He is unseen.
He was always with you,
But you were so entangled in the fleeting things of this world
That you could not hear the voice within,
The voice that warned you before every wrong decision.
God only wanted your well-being,
But you were so lost in the temporary benefits of this world

That you forgot your true journey,

Where you are but a guest for a few days."

Zarrar suddenly stood up in shock, his face filled with bewilderment. He took two steps forward and then two steps back, his mind caught in a whirlwind of emotions. His face turned pale—this was the moment, the one moment when Zarrar was finally convinced that God had always been there, and still was. His voice began to tremble, his body grew cold, and with a shaky voice, he asked, "Can God forgive me? Will Allah forgive me?"

A gentle smile appeared on the Imam's face as he replied, "No! No, God will never forgive you—until you forgive yourself. Until you lift the weight of your ego off your shoulders."

Confused, Zarrar asked, "What do you mean, sir? I don't understand."

The Imam laughed and responded, "Let go of your ego, forgive those who have wronged you, and seek forgiveness from those you have wronged. God forgives all, but if a human heart is hurt because of you, God never forgives that. Doesn't God say, 'He who is not grateful to people can never be grateful to Allah'? So how can one expect Allah to forgive them if they cannot forgive others? How can someone who harms others hope for goodness from God? Allah will forgive you, but first, you must forgive yourself."

Zarrar, stunned, smiled with relief. Lost in thought, he softly said, "I will forgive myself. I will ask God for forgiveness."

The Imam excused himself, saying he had to leave for an errand. Zarrar thanked him and kissed his hand. Then, Zarrar sat in a corner of the mosque, opened the Quran, and began reciting. He earnestly prayed for forgiveness from Allah, saying, "O Allah! I fear what will happen to me when I come to You. Please forgive me."

For the first time in a long while, Zarrar performed his prayers and recited the Quran, sincerely asking Allah for forgiveness with all his heart.

On a cool October evening, after Asr prayer, Zarrar stepped out of the mosque. His face reflected a sense of peace, yet deep down, there was still an emptiness. He had changed, but there was still something unresolved inside him. Throughout this time, his thoughts didn't drift towards Amira; instead, they were still consumed by Sawera. Lost in his thoughts, he walked ahead until he noticed a flower shop on the way.

Zarrar stopped in front of the shop and thought to himself, "I didn't go to the office today, why not take these roses for Sawera? I'll surprise her, she'll be so happy." He bought a beautiful bouquet of red roses and continued walking, a smile lighting up his face as he imagined Sawera's reaction. He was confident she'd love them.

After a while, Zarrar got into his car, thinking he would offer the Maghrib prayer at the office. Excited at the thought of giving the flowers to Sawera, he arrived at the office. He felt an odd sensation in his heart, as though this would be the last time he'd give her flowers. As he entered the office, the secretary looked at him in surprise.

"Sir! We thought you weren't coming today. Should I bring you something to eat or drink?"

Zarrar shook his head lightly, declining the offer. "Where is Sawera?"

The secretary replied, "She is in her office. Should I call her for you?"

"No, I'll go myself," Zarrar replied. Holding the flowers in his hand, he walked towards Sawera's office, thinking about how he would surprise her.

When he reached the door, he gently opened it and was taken aback to see Sawera and Adeel sitting on the couch, engaged in a conversation that seemed tense. Zarrar stepped back a little, deciding to listen to their conversation from behind the door.

Adeel:(Speaking softly, as if from the depths of his heart) "Sawera, I can't live without you. The space you've made in my life, no one else can fill. You told me Zarrar is just your boss, and I believed every word. But your eyes say something else. I feel like I'm nothing to you."

Sawera:(Taking a deep breath, averting her gaze from Adeel) "Adeel, why do you think there's something between Zarrar and me? I've always told you, he's just my boss and nothing more. I know it's difficult for you, but I'm here for you. You're important to me."

(Zarrar's face contorts with anger and pain, as he begins to realize the betrayal behind each of her words.)

Adeel: (Innocently, as though every word came from his heart) "Sawera, you don't understand how deep my love for you is. I never asked for anything except your presence. If you ask me to, I'll wait for you forever, until the day you return to me."

Sawera: (Hesitating for a moment, but quickly concealing her emotions) "Adeel, you're too sensitive. You don't understand—life isn't that simple. Sometimes, we have to make compromises. You know Zarrar is a powerful man, and I'm learning a lot from him. But that doesn't mean your place in my life is shrinking."

(Zarrar clenches his fists tightly. He still couldn't comprehend the extent to which he was merely a pawn in Sawera's game.)

Adeel: (Softly, as if clinging to a fragile hope) "Sawera, I'm willing to sacrifice everything for you. Just tell me that I truly mean something to you. You know I would never leave you, no matter what."

(Sawera's eyes flicker with unease for a moment. She knows Adeel is important to her, especially since she's aware that Zarrar may never truly be hers.)

Sawera: (Craftily, masking her emotions) "Adeel, you've always been important to me. I couldn't have done all this without you. But with Zarrar, it's purely professional. He's helping me with my work, and I need that right now. You have to understand, this is temporary."

(It's as if someone had struck Zarrar in the chest. He realized Sawera had never truly cared for him. She had only ever used him for her own needs.)

Adeel: (Smiling softly, with innocence in his love) "I want you forever, Sawera. I'll wait for as long as it takes until you need me. You know I'll never disappoint you."

Sawera: (carefully choosing her words) "Adeel, you are mine, always. No one can take you away from me, and I know you'll always be there for me."

(Zarrar's heart feels like it's shattering. He realizes Sawera has only been using him all along. He was never important to her, just a necessity—just like Adeel, who seemed like her backup plan.)

Adeel: (Struggling to keep himself together) "All I want is your truth, Sawera. I love you, but do you feel the same for me?"

Sawera: (Feeling a tinge of nervousness, as though her lies were about to be exposed) "Adeel, you don't need to worry about such things. I've told you, I'm with you. I can't live without you, but right now... it's just not the right time."

(Adeel's voice trembles as though his heart was breaking piece by piece.)

Adeel:(Speaking quietly, with every word carrying his pain) "I'll wait for you, Sawera. As long as you need me, I'll be here for you."

(Sawera's eyes gleam for a moment, as if she had secured her position. She knew Adeel would always be there for her, whether or not Zarrar stayed in her life.)

Sawera: (With a faint smile) "Adeel, you are so important to me. I know you'll always be with me. But let's drop all this for now—I'm starving. Let's go grab something to eat."

Before Adeel could respond, Zarrar's voice cut through the air from behind.

Zarrar: (Sarcastically, but with visible anger in his eyes) "So, are you two done with your conversation, or should I wait a little longer before saying something?"

The second Zarrar's voice hit their ears, both Adeel and Sawera froze in fear and shock. They stood up, panic flashing across their faces. Neither of them could believe that Zarrar had been standing there the whole time, listening to every word.

Zarrar steps forward, smiling sarcastically as he extends his hand towards Adeel for a handshake.

"How are you, Adeel?" he says, with a hint of mockery in his voice.

Adeel, taken aback, replies nervously, "I'm fine, sir."

Zarrar continues smiling, nodding. "Good, good," he says before turning to Sawera. "Oh yes, I brought these flowers for you." His smile remains, but there's an undeniable bitterness beneath it.

He places the bouquet on her desk, his mocking smile deepening, while Sawera stands there, stunned and uneasy. As Zarrar turns to leave, Sawera rushes forward in a panic. "Zarrar, listen to me, please!"

Zarrar, with fury burning in his eyes, raises his hand sharply, stopping her in her tracks. "Stay back," he commands coldly. "Get away from me."

Sawera, shaken and terrified, takes a step back, tears welling up in her eyes.

Zarrar continues towards the door, but suddenly pauses. He turns around and says, "There's a difference between you and me, Adeel."

Adeel looks at him, confused and guilty.

Zarrar's voice drips with cold disdain. "**You knew everything and still played the fool. I was the fool, not knowing.**"

He stops, his words heavy with finality. "**Next time, when you fall in love, remember—there are no excuses or compromises in love.**"

With that, he walks out of the room, leaving a stunned silence behind him.

As he steps outside, the secretary, visibly confused, approaches him. "Sir—what happened? Is everything okay?"

Zarrar, still seething with anger, interrupts her sharply. "Fire both of them. Prepare their documents. I don't want to see them in this office again after today. Or else today will be your last day too."

The secretary stands there, utterly bewildered. Just moments ago, everything seemed fine, and now everything had taken a sudden and drastic turn. She doesn't dare question Zarrar's orders and simply responds, "Yes, sir."

Zarrar, without another word, storms into his office, the fury still coursing through him.

Zarrar sat in his office, spinning in his swivel chair, his mind consumed with rage. His fists clenched, the anger he felt toward Sawera surged through him. How could she deceive him for someone as insignificant as Adeel? The thought gnawed at him—he, a powerful man, fooled by someone he had trusted.

He kept replaying the scene in his mind, Sawera's words, Adeel's blind devotion, all of it twisting his insides with fury. But then, something shifted. Another thought began creeping into his mind—*what was I doing all this time with Amira?* He whispered her name under his breath, and with it came the flood of memories he had been avoiding. The lies, the distance, the neglect—he had treated Amira with the same disregard that Sawera had shown him today.

As he sat there, replaying these thoughts, the words of the Imam from the mosque echoed in his mind, (In the love you give boundlessly to someone, yet they will reject you, and in the love someone gives you unconditionally, yet you will turn them away...) The realization hit him hard.

Suddenly, everything became clear. God was giving him a lesson through Sawera, showing him the consequences of his actions. All those years of cheating on Amira, of treating her as if she were nothing more than an obligation—God had sent him his punishment. Sawera, who he thought was his escape, had turned into a mirror reflecting his own cruelty.

Zarrar's anger began to dissolve, replaced by something heavier—disgust, not for Sawera, but for himself. He was no better. He had become the very thing he despised, playing with hearts, betraying the people who trusted him.

The Imam's words rang true— (You cannot become a king on this earth by causing pain to God's creation). God had humbled him through the same hands he had used to betray others.

Zarrar's chest tightened with shame. The realization that he had caused Amira years of pain for the same fleeting satisfaction that Sawera had offered him now made him sick to his core. His rage subsided completely, replaced by a deep sense of guilt.

For the first time in years, he felt small.

(Sawera stands in silence for a moment, still shaken by Zarrar's cold departure. Her breathing is uneven, and her mind races. She turns to Adeel, her eyes narrowing as she looks for someone to blame. Adeel stands there, looking shattered but desperate to fix the situation.)

Sawera (her voice sharp, filled with frustration): "This is all your fault, Adeel! If you hadn't kept coming to me with your stupid emotions, none of this would've happened! Zarrar was furious, and now I'm the one who has to pay for it."

Adeel (his face pale, voice trembling with guilt): "Sawera ....i'm so sorry. I never meant for this to happen. I didn't think—"

Sawera (cutting him off, her anger boiling over): "Exactly! You didn't think! All you ever do is think about yourself, your feelings. Do you even realize what you've done to me? Zarrar's going to fire me, and it's because of you!"

Adeel (his eyes filled with tears, shaking his head): "No, no... it wasn't supposed to be like this. I didn't want to hurt you, Sawera. I would never..."

Sawera (mocking, with a bitter laugh): "Never? You've ruined everything, Adeel! Zarrar means everything to me. You've destroyed my chances with him, and for what? For your selfish love?"

Adeel (desperately): "Sawera, please... don't say that. I'll fix this, I swear. I'll talk to him. I'll take all the blame. You don't have to worry, just tell him it was all my fault."

Sawera (her voice dripping with venom): "Of course, it's your fault. Zarrar trusted me, and now he thinks I've been playing him, all because of you! Why couldn't you just stay out of it?"

Adeel (pleading, his heart breaking): "I couldn't stay away... I love you, Sawera. I couldn't stand seeing you with him, knowing that I mean nothing to you. But I'll do whatever you want. Just... forgive me. Please."

Sawera (cold, with an air of superiority): "Forgive you? You think it's that easy? You've ruined everything for me, Adeel. And you expect me to just forgive you like that?"

Adeel (tears streaming down his face): "Please, Sawera. I'll take all the blame. I'll tell him it was my fault, that I forced myself on you. Just don't leave me. I'll do anything for your forgiveness, anything for your love."

Sawera (crossing her arms, her face emotionless): "You'd better. If you don't fix this, I'll make sure you're the one who's fired, not me."

Adeel (nodding frantically, his voice breaking): "I'll fix it, I promise. I'll do whatever it takes."

Sawera (finally softening, but only for her own gain): "Good. You should have thought about that before. You're lucky I even talk to you after all this."

Adeel: "I'm sorry... I'm so sorry, Sawera. I'll make it right. I swear, I'll do whatever it takes."

Sawera (calm now, in control of the situation): "You'd better. Because if I go down, I'm taking you with me."

Zarrar stood up from his chair, his face showing exhaustion and his heart burdened with a strange weight as he slowly walked out of the office.

As soon as he stepped outside the office, he took a deep breath, as if there was a heaviness in the air that was making it hard for him to breathe. When he sat in his car, only one thought echoed in his mind—Sawera had betrayed him, and that betrayal had shaken the very foundation of his life.

Driving along, he wondered how he would face Amira at home. How could he meet her eyes? The woman he had deceived for someone else, and that someone else had now deceived him. The view outside the car window seemed blurry, as though his eyes were trying to escape from his own reality.

As the sky deepened into twilight, the call for Maghrib echoed, and Zarrar made his way toward the mosque. He hoped to find a moment of peace within, something to ease the weight on his heart. Yet, as he stepped inside and took his place in the prayer line, the heaviness only seemed to grow. Thoughts circled in his mind, clouding his focus.

After completing the prayer, he walked out, but the idea of going home felt unbearable. He couldn't bring himself to face Amira. What could he possibly say to her? How could he meet her gaze after everything? Shame weighed down his soul, and his own reflection now felt foreign to him. Once more, his feet took him back to the same lonely bench in the park.

As he sat down, his body felt as heavy as his heart, the silent refrain echoing in his mind—**"Sawera betrayed me, and I betrayed myself."**

Just then, a soft voice cut through the silence. He looked up to see a young woman, passing by on her way home from the park. She wore a warm, genuine smile, her presence calm yet somehow vibrant in the dim light. She paused as she noticed Zarrar's troubled expression.

Without directly addressing his pain, she simply said, **"You know, sometimes, it's the smallest seeds that grow into the biggest, strongest trees. All they need is patience... and time."**

Her words settled in the air like the gentle rustling of leaves. With a reassuring glance, Noor walked away, leaving Zarrar with her message lingering in his mind. For a moment, he sat there, processing her words, feeling an odd comfort in their simplicity. He felt the depth in her message—perhaps everything, even his pain, had its purpose, its own quiet potential to grow into something greater.

A strange calm washed over him as he returned to the mosque, performing a heartfelt prayer, letting each word reach his core. Then, as if drained by the weight of his emotions, he returned to the bench. Without realizing it, sleep overcame him right there, as though his heart had given in to exhaustion, and now his soul sought rest.

Chapter 4: Fragments of Yesterday

At the call of the morning prayer, Zarrar wakes up. As he sits up, he recalls that he had spent the night on a bench by the side of a road. It is still completely dark, but upon hearing the call to prayer, he makes his way toward the mosque. On arriving, he performs ablution and offers two units of Sunnah prayer.

Zarrar notices that there are very few people in the mosque, yet he feels immense peace within himself. There's a strange kind of happiness in his heart, knowing that he is offering the Fajr prayer at the mosque. After completing the Sunnah, he sits quietly. Suddenly, an elderly man walks past him and takes a seat in the front row. The elder looks back at Zarrar and smiles warmly. Zarrar smiles back, as if he had wished for this moment—like he had longed to meet this elder again, and now that wish has come true.

After the prayer, they meet outside the mosque.

It is the beginning of a beautiful morning on the 22nd of October, 2024. There's a slight chill in the air, and the sun is slowly rising, casting a faint light all around. Crimson, dry leaves are scattered everywhere. Sometimes, the leaves crunch under the elder's feet, and sometimes under Zarrar's. The sounds of birds chirping fill the air, creating a lively melody. The two walk together silently, side by side.

"I've been waiting for you eagerly. There's so much I want to talk about. I have so many things to say that a whole day could pass by, but I don't have anyone to sit with and share these thoughts. Meeting you made me feel like I could talk to you about everything," Zarrar says with a smile.

The elder chuckles gently and replies softly, "My son, that's your kindness. In truth, we have many people around us too, but we often waste our emotions and words on those who don't care whether we exist or not. And maybe that's why we pour our hearts out to them—hoping they'll stay with us. But how long can a guest really stay in one's home?"

As they continue walking, Zarrar lowers his head and, with a sad smile, murmurs, "You're absolutely right... absolutely right."

They reach a nearby bench and quietly take a seat.

He sat on the bench and took a deep breath. Perhaps the time had come for him to share his story, to reveal himself.

"I was a very loving child. I cared for everyone and never hurt anyone. No matter how much I cherished something, if someone else liked it, I would give it to them. My mother used to say, 'Son, Zarrar, you are too innocent and too pure. These people won't let you live.' But I couldn't understand what she meant.

When I was 14 years old, my parents died in a car accident. My uncle, whose name was Ahmed... Ahmed Uncle..."

Zarrar smiled sadly as he said his uncle's name, as if some heavy memory had surfaced, as if he had forgotten him and suddenly remembered. He fell silent and lowered his head. After taking a deep breath, he said softly, "Ahmed Uncle took me with him to the village. That's where I saw Amira for the first time—who is now my wife.

At that time, I had no one. No friends, except Amira. And only my uncle Ahmed, who raised me, took care of me, and made sure I never felt deprived.

But still, we were very poor. There was very little food, and we didn't even have a proper place to live.

I was very weak as a child. Kids at school and in the neighborhood used to make fun of me. They bullied me, and because of my dark complexion, they gave me weird names. Everywhere I went, I faced ridicule.

Going to school was very difficult because everyone made fun of me there. I barely went outside in the neighborhood because I had no friends there either. I was always alone..."

He took a long breath, and it felt like the moment had finally arrived for him to tell his story—his truth.

"I've learned one thing in life: if you want to survive in this world, you need both looks and wealth. In fact, if you have money, even your looks will fall into place. With that in mind, I dedicated myself to hard work, and I earned a lot—so much that my desires vanished.

But now I realize I was nothing more than a mental patient. Every morning, I would exercise for two hours, and then spend just as long grooming my face and improving my complexion. But for whom? For this world that doesn't care whether I exist or not.

This is a world that has everything, yet remains depressed—a world that knows neither itself nor God, nor its own soul. And here I am, trying to please it.

'Look at me now; I look good—love me.'

'See, I have money—love me.'

'I'm not weak anymore; I have muscles now—love me.'

'I'm not dark-skinned anymore—love me.'

But do I really need their love? Does the happiness of this world even matter? I don't think so!

This world demands we become what it wants us to be, but I was fine just the way I was. What I became was nothing more than a circus performer, trying to entertain an audience by erasing my own identity. We've all become clowns, constantly changing ourselves to make others happy—until we lose sight of who we really are.

Everyone forgets themselves in this endless race to be liked by others—even by strangers passing by on the street. We shape ourselves according to their preferences, hoping they'll accept us.

This society is like a stage. People are either performers or spectators, all trapped in the same circus. Performers don't even know why they are trying to impress the audience, and the audience doesn't understand why they're watching the show.

We're all desperately trying to impress each other, but what's the point? We forget that, to a mother, her child is always the most beautiful person in the world—no matter what. But we still try to please everyone. And in the end, those very people leave us—the ones we changed ourselves for.

We overlook the fact that those who love us truly will accept us as we are. But instead, we keep changing ourselves for others and, in doing so, lose our identity.

Women wear makeup every day—why? To look beautiful? But why is beauty even necessary? Why can't someone love them just the way they are?

Why do I need to wake up every morning, shave, work out, and build six-pack abs? Why must I meet the world's standards just to be liked?

Why do we surround ourselves with people who only stay with us if we keep giving them reasons to? Yes, people cry when we die—but do we have anyone in our lives who truly loves us? No.

We are all dancing in this circus. And when the show ends, no one will care.

As Zarrar spoke, his voice grew louder with every sentence. His hands gripped the bench tightly, his voice trembled, and his eyes were bloodshot—on the verge of tears. Though he hadn't cried yet, it seemed like the tears could fall any moment.

He stopped and bowed his head, but then suddenly, he began to laugh.

"We are strange people," he said with a bitter chuckle. "So strange. We chase beauty as if it's something divine. But as soon as the body is stripped of its adornments, that beauty fades within moments.

But there is one thing that never fades—the heart within that body.

We are strange because we know how to measure beauty, but not the worth of a heart. People don't seek hearts anymore—they are obsessed only with appearances. They either know how to put a price on beauty or on the clothes that cover it.

Only a handful of people recognize the value of a heart, and they leave behind beautiful stories when they depart from this world. But people like us, hungry for beauty and appearances, dismiss such stories, saying, 'That only happens in fairy tales.'

In my pursuit of the world's approval, I abandoned the people who truly wanted to be with me. I left them behind, thinking I needed to earn the love of this world. I believed that I could never have a real friend.

In chasing money, I betrayed my friends. I overlooked the people who loved me, kept them in the dark, and deceived them. I wasn't always like this—I was good once. But to become what the world wanted, I did everything it demanded. We don't really want anything for ourselves in this world. We live just to make others happy. The way we walk, the money we earn, the houses we build, the big cars we buy, People marry and fall in love with beautiful individuals just so others can say, "Look how lucky they are to have such a beautiful partner." it's all done so that people praise us and talk about us. It's all deception, just an illusion. We're constantly busy trying to please and impress those around us. Nothing we do here is truly for ourselves, and I fell victim to this disease too. What have I done?

What have I done?"

Zarrar looked at the old man, his eyes filled with regret. "What have I done? What have I done?"

The elder looks at Zarrar with astonishment, wondering what this young man has just said. When Zarrar finishes speaking and falls silent, the elder too remains quiet for a few moments. Then, turning towards Zarrar, he says, "Perhaps you're right... No, surely you are right... Yes, absolutely, you are right."

The elder coughs again, a deep, tired cough, as if it carried the weight of his life's burdens. He shifts uncomfortably on the bench and gazes at the trees ahead. After a moment of silence, he begins to speak slowly, as if peeling back the layers of his soul. The elder begins telling his story once again, but he doesn't have the habit of forgetting.

"I was a government servant for forty years. My life was never about me; it was always for my children. My wife passed away when our sons were still young. She was only thirty. I didn't have time to mourn her; I had to become both a mother and a father to my boys. I gave up everything for them—my dreams, my health, and even my happiness. Every extra penny I earned was for their education, their comfort. If they wanted something, I made sure they had it, no matter what. I denied myself so that they wouldn't feel the absence of their mother.

I borrowed money—so much money—because I wanted them to have the best education, the best life. I thought they would repay my sacrifices with love, that one day, they would be proud of me. But as they grew older, the distance between us also grew. They never understood the sleepless nights, the weight of the loans, or the silent battles I fought for them. They only saw what they wanted from me.

Now, I live like a beggar in the very homes I built for them. They pass me around like an unwanted burden—two months with one son, two months with the other. I sit quietly in their homes, watching their lives unfold, hoping for some kindness. But there's no room for kindness when all they see is an old man who has nothing left to offer.

I took loans—so many loans—for their education and weddings. And now, I can't even pay them back. I am drowning in debt, but it's not just the debt that weighs me down—it's the indifference of the very children I starved myself for. They argue over whose turn it is to take me in, not out of love but out of obligation. They don't ask how I'm doing; they ask how much longer I'll live. On Eid, instead of celebrating together, they fight over who will have to deal with me or how to divide my property after I'm gone.

They don't even offer me three meals a day. That's why I spend most of my time here, in the park. Every morning, I leave for Fajr prayer and don't return until after Zuhr. At home, there's only loneliness and silence waiting for me. I have a heart condition, and I know one day my heart will simply stop beating in my sleep. But I doubt anyone will notice right away.

This is life, son. You give everything you have to those you love, but in the end, you're left with nothing. Parents are respected only as long as they're providing. The moment they become a burden, they are discarded. That's the truth of this world—your worth only lasts as long as you are useful."

The elder sighs deeply and says, "And Yes — Yes — People enroll their children in big, expensive schools not for the sake of a better education but so others will see and praise them. It's all a facade—this idea that those schools provide better learning. The truth is, it's not about education; it's about status. Parents want to flaunt that their children go to elite institutions, as if it somehow elevates their own worth in society.

This world teaches us from the very beginning that appearances matter more than reality. We buy things we don't need, live in houses we can't afford, and even raise our children according to what society expects of us. Everything becomes a performance—a spectacle for the world to admire. And by the time we realize the futility of it all, it's often too late."

Zarrar listens intently, each word of the elder hitting him like a painful truth. He reflects on his own life, realizing how much of his journey has been dictated by the need to impress others.

The elder continues, "What they don't tell you is that no matter how much you try, someone will always have more—more money, more success, more admiration. And those who chase these things end up with nothing that truly matters. Relationships become transactions, and love is reduced to comparisons. Even children become trophies, paraded not for who they are, but for what they represent—a family's status in the eyes of society. We are merely wandering around, trying to please one another. Have we ever even thought about whether we ourselves are truly happy? It's a strange kind of war where everyone claims to love each other, yet no one calls it a war. With sweet words, they are busy looting each other's treasures."

A silence falls between them again, as if the forest itself is absorbing their words. Both men sit, lost in thought, realizing that the race to impress the world is a race without a finish line.

Zarrar turns and asks in amazement, "How much debt do you have?"

The elder replies sorrowfully, "What could I have managed with a government job? I had to pay for my children's education and build a house. I kept borrowing, and now I owe 2 million rupees. People come to me sometimes, hinting that I might not return their money, but out of respect, they don't say it directly. But the truth is, I owe them their money, and I have nothing left to repay them. The shame is there, but the greatest fear is that one day, I'll have to answer to my Lord. And that fear never leaves me."

Zarrar, with a reassuring tone, says, "Don't worry, everything will be fine."

The elder nods and says, "Let me go home today; I'm not feeling too well."

Zarrar quickly responds, "Of course, please take care. If it's serious, we can go to the doctor."

The elder replies gently, "No, it's not that serious, just a little fatigue."

The elder stands, and Zarrar rises to accompany him.

The elder bids farewell and starts to leave.

Suddenly, Zarrar asks, "What's your name? I haven't even asked you yet."

The elder turns back and smiles, saying, **"People admire you as long as they don't know you. Once they do, they only humiliate you."**

Zarrar chuckles and lowers his head, saying, "You're absolutely right. But at least tell me where your house is."

The elder replies, "It's just behind this park."

As the elder walks away, Zarrar calls out loudly from behind,

"Dad.! —— I love you, Dad.———"

Zarrar says it with excitement and joy, smiling.

The elder turns around, smiling warmly, as if those words brought him immense happiness.

Raising the hand holding his walking stick, he waves goodbye with a smile.

Zarrar stands there, watching until the elder disappears down the road.

Zarrar sits back on the bench, and suddenly, he remembers that tomorrow is his last day. Instantly, the thought strikes him that it's time to seek forgiveness for his mistakes. Without wasting a moment, he gets up and heads toward the office.

When he arrives at the office, everyone looks at him with surprise. His beard is overgrown since he hasn't shaved for two days. He is wearing the same black suit, even though Zarrar was known for never repeating his clothes. The suit, too, is dirty and covered with dust.

As he makes his way toward his room, his secretary rushes to him, looking concerned.

"Sir! Where have you been? We've been trying to contact you for so long. Your phone was off, too."

Zarrar smiles warmly and says, "I'm fine, Anum. Please come to my room; I need to have a meeting with you."

With that, the two head to the room for the meeting.

Zarrar sits at the head of the conference table, stacks of documents neatly arranged before him. His secretary sits across from him, anxiously watching every move he makes. The room is eerily quiet, with only the scratching sound of the pen as Zarrar signs papers—one after another—dividing his shares, assets, and property.

His expression is calm, almost detached, as if the significance of his actions doesn't weigh on him. The secretary's unease grows with each signature he completes. She can't comprehend why a man so meticulous about his wealth would be giving it all away.

Finally, as Zarrar slides the last signed document into a folder, the secretary, unable to hold back any longer, softly asks, "Sir, why are you doing this?"

Zarrar looks up briefly, a faint, melancholic smile forming on his lips. **"This is nothing to me,"** he replies. "There are people who deserve it more."

Without another word, Zarrar gathers the documents in his hands, rises from the chair, and walks out of the office. His footsteps echo through the empty hall, leaving the Anum sitting alone, stunned and confused by what just transpired.

Zarrar sits in his car and drives off, determined to visit his friend and ask for forgiveness. His friend lives near Zarrar's old house, and Zarrar has also the keys to his childhood home, intending to go there.

After a short drive, he arrives at his destination and catches sight of the house where he spent his early years with his uncle. Seeing the house after so many years leaves him feeling both amazed and unsettled. He pulls the keys from the ignition and begins walking slowly towards the house.

Zarrar closes his car door and drives towards the old house. Memories begin pulling him into the past as the streets blur by. When he arrives, he pauses, staring at the house that holds his childhood—his life with his uncle and Amira. Taking a deep breath, he pulls out the old keys, and as the door creaks open, the sound pierces his soul. **It's the same creak** from their childhood, back when it was part of their games. **"Remember who can open the door with less noise?"** His laughter and Amira's teasing echoes in his mind, now twisting painfully inside him.

Stepping in, the air is thick with memories. Each wall and corner seems alive, dragging him back to the past. As he moves towards the staircase, a flood of memories crashes over him. **Amira had hidden under the stairs,** and Zarrar searched for her, grinning. Her laughter feels like it still lingers in the walls. **"Amira, you lost!"** His voice rings in his ears, followed by their laughter when she pretended to be upset.

He climbs the stairs and reaches the room where he and his uncle used to watch movies. The **same old sofa** waits, frozen in time. Sitting down, Zarrar recalls how they spent every weekend watching films, laughing and sharing jokes. **"This movie is great!"** his uncle would say, and Zarrar would nestle close, feeling safe and happy.

But the memories don't stop. He remembers the day **Amira fell off her bike and scraped her knee.** Zarrar still feels that moment as if it were yesterday. **"Don't cry, here's my handkerchief... the bleeding will stop."** Amira's innocent, trusting face flashes before him, warming and breaking his heart all at once.

He also remembers **their childhood fights—how she pinched him, and he shoved her back.** They ended up in trouble, their uncle scolding them both, only to laugh later, saying, **"You two will never change!"**

The kitchen door catches his eye. He remembers the time **Amira spilled milk while making tea. "Told you, you can't make tea!"** he teased, and she angrily threw the cup at him. Moments later, they sat on the floor, laughing uncontrollably.

Each step, each wall, carries another piece of his soul. His heart feels heavy. His **eyes are red, brimming with unshed tears.** Sitting on the stairs, he cradles his head in his hands. **Memories swirl around him,** his uncle's scolding, Amira's laughter, their fights—it all feels overwhelming.

"Where did I get lost?" he whispers, as if pleading with the past to answer. Then comes the memory of **Eid,** when he raced down these same stairs shouting, **"The moon is out! The moon is out!"** He and Amira celebrated together, hugging their uncle. He recalls how **Amira sneakily applied Mehndi on his feet,** only for him to yell at her the next morning—but they both laughed it off.

Zarrar tries to stand, but **the weight of memories** pulls him down. He collapses on the stairs, crying out, **"Forgive me! Forgive me!"** His voice echoes through the house, filling the silence. **Every wall seems to listen, every corner a witness to his torment.**

Suddenly, he springs to his feet, rushes to the door, and steps outside. Wiping his face hurriedly, he whispers, **"I need to see Uncle... I need to see him."** Without wasting a second, he **runs towards the cemetery**, his breath ragged, but he doesn't stop. **He runs... and keeps running...**

Zarrar races into the cemetery, heart pounding and eyes searching. He looks for his uncle's grave, each step echoing with memories. Finally, he spots a grave with his uncle's name engraved on it. Upon seeing it, his face pales, and tears stream down his cheeks. He collapses beside the grave, placing his hands on the cool stone, and begins to weep loudly. This is the first time he allows himself to cry.

"Forgive me, Uncle!" he cries out. **"I didn't fulfill my promise. Please forgive me!"** His voice breaks, but he continues to repeat, **"Forgive me! — Forgive me! "** But, what promise?

He remembers how, as his uncle was nearing the end, he said, "**Do me one favor, marry my daughter; she has no one but you.**" Zarrar and Amira knew that his uncle might not see another day, so despite his reluctance, Zarrar married Amira. Just before passing, his uncle called Zarrar and said, "**Promise me you'll always take care of Amira.**" Zarrar promised, and that was their last conversation. Soon after, his uncle departed from this world.

Now, Zarrar sits by his uncle's grave, "**Uncle! Forgive me! I didn't keep my promise! Forgive me, Uncle. I buried myself in my ego and neglected the one promise you asked me to keep.**" He whispers, the words barely escaping his lips. "**Please forgive me! I didn't repay your kindness!**" He cries, pouring out his heart, losing track of time.

After a moment of silence, he finally speaks, "**Uncle, I haven't fulfilled my promise, but I will fix my mistake. I will apologize to Amira.**" He wipes his tears and stands tall, determination shining through his sorrow.

"**I will make things right, Uncle!**" he declares, starting to turn away but stopping to say, "**I'm coming back, Uncle! I'm coming back!**" With that, Zarrar wipes his tears one last time and walks away from the grave, a newfound hope guiding his steps.

Zarrar steps out of his car and walks towards the front door, a sense of fear and unease gripping his heart. He wonders if Ali will forgive him, unsure of how he'll face him after all these years. Zarrar knocks on the door, and while waiting for a response, the anxiety within him grows stronger.

A woman's voice calls from inside, "Who is it?"

Zarrar pauses, struggling to find the right words.

When there's no immediate answer, the woman asks again, "Who's there?"

Without thinking, Zarrar blurts out, "It's Zarrar... Ali's friend."

The door opens, and a woman steps out, looking at him with surprise. "You're Zarrar?" she asks.

Zarrar nods nervously. "Yes... I need to meet Ali."

The woman responds, "He's at the office right now, but he'll be back soon. Please, come inside and have a seat."

Zarrar hesitantly steps inside and sits on the couch.

present nor ready to give way to evening. Sunlight filters through half-drawn curtains, casting soft, golden beams on the wooden floor. Dust motes float lazily in the air, visible only where the light falls, as if time itself has slowed to match the mood of the hour.

At the center of the room is a deep brown leather sofa, worn with age, its creases telling stories of years gone by. Zarrar sits on it, leaning slightly forward with his elbows resting on his knees, hands loosely clasped together. The cushions are a little off-kilter, as if someone had tried to arrange them hastily but stopped midway. A soft throw blanket dangles unevenly over the armrest, one corner brushing against the floor.

The room carries the faint aroma of old furniture, blended with the subtle scent of jasmine from a diffuser sitting on a nearby side table. On the table rests a glass of water, untouched, the condensation leaving a faint ring—a silent reminder of its prolonged presence. Next to it lies an open notebook with hurried scribbles, a pen tucked between its pages, as though someone had abandoned a thought midway and never returned to finish it.

The walls are painted in a soft beige, lending the room a warm, cozy hue, though the silence hanging in the air feels heavy—like the room has absorbed memories that no one speaks of aloud. A large clock ticks steadily on the wall, its sound amplified in the stillness, marking each second louder than necessary. Below the clock is a shelf filled with books, framed photographs, and small keepsakes, giving the room a personal, intimate feel—a place where the past and present seem to coexist in quiet harmony.

Ali's wife brings him a glass of water and, with a mix of joy and hesitation, says, "Not a single day went by when Ali didn't mention you. All the time, he'd talk about his friend Zarrar—'He used to do this, he would say that.' I got tired of hearing your name, but Ali never told me where you disappeared."

A faint smile flickers on Zarrar's lips, but sorrow lingers in his eyes. He lowers his head, clasping his hands together in a nervous gesture, as if struggling to hide his anxiety.

Just then, Ali walks into the room.

"Zarrar?!" Ali exclaims in disbelief.

Zarrar stands up, offering a small, melancholic smile, and nods. "Assalamu Alaikum!"

Ali replies to the greeting, stunned by Zarrar's appearance. The disheveled beard and dust-covered clothes tell Ali that something serious has happened.

When Ali's wife sees them together, she quietly leaves the room.

Ali sits on the sofa beside Zarrar, and Zarrar, too, takes a seat next to him.

A silence falls between them. Ali, noticing Zarrar's condition, asks, "What have you done to yourself, Zarrar?"

Zarrar shakes his head with a faint smile and says, "It's nothing, Brother."

Ali, puzzled, asks, "Is everything okay, Zarrar?"

Zarrar smiles again and replies, "Yeah, everything is fine, Brother."

But Zarrar couldn't gather the courage to say what he wanted to tell Ali.

Ali begins, "After all this time..." but Zarrar cuts him off, saying, "Forgive me, brother. Please forgive me, my brother."

Ali looks at Zarrar in disbelief. "Forgiveness? And you're asking for it?"

Zarrar gives a weak smile and replies, "Yes, my brother, forgive me. I did you wrong."

Ali stares at him. "Do you even know what you did to me, Zarrar? I trusted you, and you betrayed me. I know greed can make people selfish, but couldn't you see the friend standing in front of you—your childhood friend?"

Zarrar lowers his head in shame and says, "Say whatever you want. I'll listen to everything today."

Ali's voice sharpens. "What should I even say, Zarrar? I loved you like a brother. And you stabbed me in the back. Where was I supposed to go? Who was I supposed to tell my sorrows to? You made me fall in people's eyes—the same people who I used to tell you were the best in the world. And then you ruined me in front of the whole world."

Ali's voice cracks, and tears fill his eyes. "I had nothing to eat, no place to stay. Do you know I couldn't even face my mother that day? She used to praise you all the time. What could I have told her, Zarrar? That the one you consider your son left your real son to beg for survival?"

There's a deep ache in Ali's voice, and he steps closer to Zarrar. **"You know, it doesn't hurt when you realize someone has betrayed you. It hurts when it's the person you loved the most in this world who does it."**

Hearing this, Zarrar lifts his head, his eyes now misty.

Ali looks into Zarrar's eyes and continues, "I couldn't sleep for a whole week after that. I kept complaining to God, asking Him why He had to take everything from me through the hands of the person dearest to me."

Ali's voice takes on a mournful tone. "A commander enters the battlefield with pride and determination, believing no force in the world can defeat him.

But do you know what breaks a commander's pride and spirit? What strips him and his army bare on the battlefield? It's betrayal. Betrayal shatters a commander, not just in the eyes of his troops but in his own eyes. **A man doesn't die when death comes for him; he dies when he falls in his own eyes.** That's the day he is truly defeated, and that's the day he changes."

Zarrar listens, his face filled with regret and shame. Ali stands up and looks down at him.

"Never break someone's pride, Zarrar," Ali says with sorrow. **"Kill a man if you must, but don't shatter his pride."**

Zarrar listens with his head bowed, knowing he was in the wrong. Taking a deep breath, he rises slowly and says softly, "It's strange, A man can go to great lengths to do something wrong, but when it comes to asking for forgiveness, he's only left with one sentence: **'Forgive me.'** Ali, I made a grave mistake, and all I can ask is for your forgiveness. I can't give you back the years you lost, but I can do something for the years ahead. Just forgive me."

With that, Zarrar kneels to grab Ali's feet, but Ali immediately pulls him up and embraces him tightly.

"Enough, Brother! I love you. How could I not forgive you?" Ali says through tears, hugging Zarrar tightly. Both friends hold each other, crying, as Zarrar repeatedly whispers, "Forgive me, Brother. Please forgive me."

Ali pulls back and wipes Zarrar's tears. "That's enough, brother. Just don't do anything like this again."

Zarrar, wiping his own tears and smiling through them, says, "I didn't just come here to ask for forgiveness."

He laughs softly, picks up a file from the table, and hands it to Ali.

Ali looks at it in confusion and asks, "What's this?"

Zarrar replies, "It's your share, brother. It's your patience, your hard work."

Ali stares at him in disbelief. "What do you mean?"

Zarrar smiles. "These are the shares of my company. Half of it—50 percent—is now yours."

Ali's eyes widen in shock. "What are you saying, brother?"

Zarrar chuckles. "Check for yourself, You know me."

Ali opens the file again, his hands trembling with emotion. His eyes reflect disbelief and overwhelming feelings.

He looks at Zarrar as if the moment is unreal. "Zarrar, what are you doing? You came after so many years to ask for forgiveness, and now this? Why are you giving me these shares?"

With a gentle smile, Zarrar replies, "I can never repay you for the damage I caused. These shares have always been yours. My success was never mine alone—it was built on your hard work. I just didn't give you the right you deserved. But now, better late than never, I want to make things right."

Ali stays silent for a moment, trying to process his emotions. Then, he closes the file and takes a deep breath.

"Zarrar, I didn't need money or shares. All I ever wanted was for you to acknowledge what you did to me. And today, you did something I never imagined you would."

In a soft voice, Zarrar says, "I just want to stand by you now, Ali. I want to make things right. No matter what, you'll always be my brother."

Tears fill Ali's eyes again—this time, tears of gratitude and love. He steps closer and embraces Zarrar once more.

"Enough, Brother. You've given me everything back... You gave me my heart back," Ali says with a smile.

Zarrar, overwhelmed with emotion, hugs Ali even tighter. For a moment, the two friends forget all the pain, betrayal, and scars of the past.

Ali grins through his tears and says, "And listen—if you ever try doing anything without me again, I'll come straight to your house and drag you out!"

Zarrar laughs, "Deal, brother. From now on, we're in this together—work and life, both!"

The two friends laugh together, their tears mingling with smiles, as they begin a new chapter—leaving behind the bitterness of the past and looking forward to a future filled with friendship and hope.

Chapter 5: Whispers of Regret

The air is heavy with the hum of the city—cars honking, engines revving, and people hurrying to get somewhere. Zarrar's car idles at a red light, and his gaze wanders through the windshield. Across the street, a park comes into view—laughter floats in the air as children run freely, their carefree joy standing in stark contrast to the stress and suffocation of the traffic around him.

For a moment, Zarrar feels like an outsider peeking into a different world—one where time moves slower, where life is lighter. Without thinking twice, he pulls his car to the side of the road. He kills the engine, steps out, and walks toward the park, drawn by the sound of children laughing and the sight of colorful swings moving with the breeze.

As Zarrar steps onto the grass, the world feels different—quieter in some ways, livelier in others. The rustling of leaves in the wind replaces the honking of cars. The rubbery scent of playground equipment mixes with the faint sweetness of blooming flowers. Small feet patter across the soft earth, and bursts of giggles fill the air like little fireworks of joy.

Zarrar finds himself smiling for no reason—an unplanned, genuine smile, one he hasn't felt in a long time. He stands there for a few moments, watching the children play. A small boy, balancing on one foot with his arms spread wide, stumbles and laughs uncontrollably as he falls to the ground. A little girl zooms down the slide, her shrieks of delight echoing through the park.

Without hesitation, Zarrar walks to the play area, his shoes sinking slightly into the soft, damp grass. A group of kids playing tag catches sight of him.

"Uncle, you play with us!" one of them shouts, tugging at his hand.

Zarrar laughs, crouching slightly to meet their height. "Alright, but no cheating!" he teases, joining their game of tag with the enthusiasm of a child.

Soon, he's running after them, dodging swings, and laughing harder than he has in years. The weight of life seems to lift as he moves freely with the kids. His coat feels too formal now, so he takes it off, tossing it on a nearby bench without a second thought.

Moments later, Zarrar's at the slide, grinning like a kid, daring himself to go down. With a slight push, he slides down, arms raised, feeling the air rush against his face. The kids cheer as he lands with a thud, and he bursts out laughing along with them.

The golden sun hangs low in the sky, casting long shadows across the park. A gentle breeze carries the sound of laughter far and wide, blending with the rustling of trees. The swings creak softly as children glide back and forth. Every moment here feels like a brief escape from the demands of the world—like Zarrar has stepped into a bubble where responsibility can't follow.

As he sits on the grass, catching his breath with the kids sprawled around him, Zarrar realizes how foreign and yet familiar this joy feels—simple, effortless, and unfiltered. It's a kind of happiness he hadn't realized he was missing.

Eventually, the sun begins to sink, and parents call their children back home. The playground starts to empty, and the sounds grow quieter. Zarrar stands up, brushing off his pants, his heart lighter and his soul rejuvenated.

He retrieves his coat from the bench, but for a moment, he just holds it in his hand, reluctant to put it back on—as if wearing it again would mean carrying the same old burdens.

With one last glance at the now-empty swings, Zarrar walks back toward his car. But as he drives away, a soft smile lingers on his lips. He knows now that joy isn't lost—it's just waiting to be found in unexpected places.

As Zarrar heads back home, he spots the same elderly beggar he once warned harshly, threatening to break his bones if he dared come near his car. But today, Zarrar's heart is heavy with a newfound humility. He stops his car, steps out, and approaches the old man, extending a handful of money. "Forgive me," Zarrar says quietly, his voice choked with sincerity. The beggar's wrinkled face softens, and he takes the money with a gentle nod. He looks deep into Zarrar's eyes and says, **"Son, wealth and pride are like dust on the road. The more you cling to them, the more they blind you. But remember, only those willing to kneel and humble themselves can truly see the path ahead."** The words settle in Zarrar's soul, and he feels a strange calm, as though a weight he didn't know he carried has lifted. The beggar smiles, a knowing look in his eyes, before turning to leave, disappearing into the crowd with the quiet dignity of one who needs no riches.

Zarrar pulls into the driveway just as dusk settles over the city. The sky is a deep shade of indigo, with streaks of orange still clinging to the horizon. Streetlights have begun to flicker on, casting long shadows across the front of his grand house. The tall, wrought-iron gate swings open with a metallic groan, and the guard nods in greeting. Zarrar waves absently, his heart thudding slightly as reality sets back in—he has to face Amira now.

His car rolls under the porch, where soft garden lights illuminate the lush hedges lining the driveway. It's quiet except for the faint hum of cicadas and the occasional rustle of leaves in the evening breeze. He parks the car, turning off the engine, but for a moment, he doesn't move. The joy he felt just an hour ago—laughing with children, sliding down playground equipment like a carefree soul—now feels distant.

He leans back into the seat for a second, inhaling deeply. The scent of damp grass and the memory of children's laughter still linger on him, but those happy thoughts dissolve as the weight of reality returns. **What am I going to tell Amira?** The question churns in his mind. He knows the barrage of questions is waiting for him inside.

Zarrar finally opens the door and steps out. A cool breeze brushes against him, making him shiver slightly—not from the cold, but from the anxiety creeping in. The house in front of him, with its tall, arched windows and warm, glowing lights, feels almost too big, too quiet.

He adjusts his collar, brushing off a smudge of dirt from his shirt. The playful mud stains from the park are still on his shoes, and his unkempt hair carries the scent of an evening spent outdoors. The sound of his footsteps echoes softly as he walks toward the front door, each step heavy with unease.

"How do I explain this? he mutters under his breath, a nervous smile flickering across his face.

As he reaches the entrance, the house feels both inviting and intimidating. A large chandelier casts a soft golden glow in the foyer, while shadows dance along the high walls. The hum of the indoor fountain at the far end of the hall adds a strange serenity to the space, but Zarrar's heart isn't calm.

He exhales slowly, brushing a hand through his hair, and puts on the best version of a relaxed smile he can manage."Here we go."

He pushes the door open, and the scent of jasmine from the indoor plants greets him, mingling with the aroma of dinner cooking in the distance. Before he can take another step inside, he hears the familiar sound of footsteps rushing toward him.

"Zarrar!, Amira's voice pierces the air. He freezes for a moment, bracing himself, as if the warmth and ease of the park have evaporated completely.

"Zarrar! Where were you?"

Her voice is filled with a mix of worry and frustration. **"I called you so many times! Sent you messages! Where have you been? And... what happened to you? Why do you look like this?"**

Zarrar glances down at himself for the first time. His black suit is covered in dirt, his shoes caked with mud, his hair disheveled, and an unkempt beard shadowing his face. He looks like someone who has been rolling in dust and wandering aimlessly.

The barrage of questions unsettles him, and his words falter.

"I was... just at the office, busy with some work."

His voice lacks conviction, and the lie feels clumsy even to him. He meets Amira's gaze for a second, and for the first time, he feels a strange sense of fear—fear of his own wife.

"Where is your phone?"

Her tone sharpens.

Zarrar fumbles through his pockets and pulls out his phone. The screen is dark.

"It must've run out of battery," he mumbles, forcing a smile that barely conceals the tension in his voice.

Amira watches him closely, her eyes scanning his face as if she's searching for hidden truths in his words.

"Are you okay, Zarrar?" she asks, her voice quieter now but heavy with concern.

Zarrar stretches out his arms, trying to appear normal, and smiles awkwardly.

"I'm fine, see? I'm standing right here in front of you."

But even in that smile, there is unease—like someone masking a storm inside. Desperate to change the subject, Zarrar adds:

"Forget all that. Tell me, what's for dinner? I'm starving. Make something delicious."

Amira stands silently, still trying to make sense of his strange behavior.

"I made biryani... You go freshen up, I'll set the table."

"Great! I'll be back in a minute," Zarrar says quickly and heads towards his room.

Amira watches him leave, a knot of confusion tightening in her chest. Something about Zarrar's demeanor feels off. His words, his smile, his entire presence—everything seems slightly out of place.

"What's wrong with Zarrar?" she whispers to herself, unable to shake the unsettling feeling.

Zarrar sits at the dining table as a steaming plate of biryani is placed in front of him, its aroma spreading across the room like a gentle invitation. Without hesitation, he fills his plate to the brim, as if he hasn't eaten for days. He devours the food in large mouthfuls, the clinking of the spoon against the plate echoing in the quiet room.

Across from him, Amira sits, watching him in stunned silence. Her eyes carry a mix of confusion and curiosity. Zarrar seems entirely engrossed in his meal, oblivious to her gaze, as if nothing else exists in that moment. Amira finally breaks the silence, softly asking, **"Zarrar... are you okay?"**

Zarrar pauses, glances up mid-bite, his mouth still stuffed with food. He mumbles awkwardly, "Yes, yes, I'm fine." Some bits of food fall from his mouth, and Amira can't help but laugh. "Yeah, I can *see* that," she says, trying to hold back her amusement.

Zarrar smiles back sheepishly, still chewing, his cheeks full like a child caught sneaking sweets. He tries to act normal, but inside, he's restless—unsure how to start the conversation that's been brewing in his mind.

After finishing his meal, he quietly rises from the table and walks to his room. Amira remains seated, her expression still a mix of amusement and bewilderment.

In his room, Zarrar sits on the edge of the bed, releasing a deep sigh. His thoughts are racing:

"She'll come later to leave water by my bed... that's when I'll talk to her. Yes, she'll come for sure. That'll be my chance."

The night feels heavy with anticipation, and Zarrar knows that once Amira enters his room, everything will change. Or at least, he hopes it will.

Zarrar glances at the clock, realizing there's still time before Amira comes. His mind swirls with thoughts—there are things he knows he shouldn't tell Amira right now, but then again, how will she know if he doesn't?

Caught in this dilemma, an idea suddenly strikes him: *Why not write a letter?* The thought grips his mind, and without hesitation, he decides to go through with it. He opens the drawer, takes out a pen and a sheet of paper, and sits on the bed to start writing.

He writes, scratches things out, and starts over again, trying to find the right words. After several attempts, he finally gets it just right and copies the message onto a clean sheet of paper. Time seems to slip away unnoticed as he folds the letter.

Just as he finishes, there's a knock on the door. Zarrar freezes for a moment, panic settling in. He quickly jumps off the bed, frantically looking around for a place to hide the letter.

"One minute!" he shouts, trying to buy time.

He paces around the room anxiously before finally slipping the letter under his pillow. Taking a deep breath, he straightens himself in the middle of the room and calls out, "Come in."

Amira steps inside. She had already noticed something strange about Zarrar's behavior, and now he seems even more off. She glances around the room and quietly says, "I... brought you some water."

Zarrar, still jittery, responds hastily, "Yes, yes, just put it there."

She places the glass on the side table, but her eyes roam the room with mild suspicion. Zarrar watches her closely, thinking how to begin the conversation. He steps toward the bed, and Amira turns to leave.

Just then, their eyes meet—Zarrar stops, and so does Amira. A moment of silent understanding passes between them, as if both know something important is about to happen.

"I need to talk to you," Zarrar says softly.

Amira hesitates for a moment, then responds, "Yes... what is it?"

"Come, sit here," Zarrar gestures toward the bed. "We'll talk."

Amira stares at him in confusion but slowly walks over. Zarrar has already seated himself, and he pats the space next to him. She hurriedly sits beside him, leaving just a bit of distance between them—close enough to talk, but far enough to keep the tension in the air.

Zarrar's mind spins with tangled thoughts, unsure where to begin or how to frame his words. The room feels heavy with silence, as if time itself has come to a halt. Both sit quietly—Zarrar lost in confusion, and Amira overwhelmed with unease. A troubling thought gnaws at her: *What if Zarrar is about to end things between us?*

After a long pause, Zarrar finally breaks the silence, his voice trembling with hesitation and fear.

"Do you love me?"

Amira jolts as if struck by lightning. She had never expected such a question. Stunned, she springs up from the bed, her steps unsteady, and stammers, "W-What are you saying?" Her voice quivers, as if she's hiding something.

Zarrar watches her closely, his face painted with surprise. He stands up as well, concerned.

"Did I say something wrong?"

"No, I mean... you don't usually talk like this." Amira's voice is shaky, her words rushed. She looks like someone caught off guard, experiencing something completely out of the ordinary. "Maybe you're not feeling well. You should rest... I'll leave."

Her gaze drops, and her face reflects a mix of embarrassment and fear. She's blushing, but there's a nervousness beneath it, as if she's grappling with emotions she doesn't understand.

Zarrar steps forward gently, sensing her fear. He grips her arms softly and says, "Nothing's wrong... Everything is fine." His voice grows firmer, reassuring. "Sit down with me."

Amira's eyes lock onto Zarrar's, her expression filled with both wonder and confusion. *What is happening today?* She feels lost but slowly sits back down beside him.

They sit quietly, side by side on the edge of the bed, their legs dangling. Time seems to stand still, and the only thing that remains is the heavy silence between them.

The night has gently embraced the room, and the yellow glow of two bedside lamps spreads warmth into the space, softening every shadow. The lamps cast a dim, honeyed light that bathes the bed and walls, giving the room a cozy, intimate feel. Through the open window, a cool October breeze drifts in, carrying with it the scent of dry leaves and crisp air. The sheer curtains flutter gently with the breeze, creating soft ripples of motion against the quiet night. The fan hums slowly above, its steady rhythm blending with the occasional rustling of leaves from outside.

Zarrar and Amira sit side by side on the edge of the bed, their feet bare, lightly brushing the cool floor. The soft yellow light reflects off Zarrar's white kurta, making it shimmer faintly, while Amira's deep purple dress hugs her gently, the fabric shifting slightly as she breathes. The color contrasts beautifully—his white attire almost glowing in the dim light, while hers feels like twilight itself, wrapping her in a mysterious charm.

Zarrar gathered his courage, as if he were about to unburden years of weight from his heart. In a voice soft with guilt and hesitation, he began:

"It's been tjree years since we got married, Amira... and today, for the first time, you've spent more than two minutes in my room while I'm here. For the first time, you're sitting with me on this bed. For the first time, I want to talk to you... And for the first time, I touched you."

He paused briefly, choosing his words carefully, as if each word carried the weight of a long-buried regret:

"I never saw you as my wife. Not even once did I love you. I never spoke to you with affection... Not even for a day. I never once looked at you the way a husband looks at his wife—with love."

There was shame and remorse in Zarrar's eyes. Helplessly, he turned to his right and looked at Amira, sitting quietly beside him. His eyes were filled with tears, glistening under the dim light, and his face flushed with emotion. In a voice full of vulnerability, as if surrendering completely, he asked:

"Do you love me?"

There was a deep ache in his voice—an ache born from three years of unspoken emotions.

Their eyes met, and in that moment, it felt as if all the unspoken distances between them had vanished. The air between them was thick with emotions, vibrating with things left unsaid. Amira's loose hair swayed slightly in the breeze coming through the open window, and her tear-filled brown eyes shimmered in the warm glow of the room.

She let out a soft sob, as if that question had been weighing on her heart for years. With a faint smile and tears still lingering in her eyes, she said:

"You said it so easily... Do you love me?"

There was a bittersweetness in her smile—a blend of complaint, affection, and relief. It was as though all the years of confusion were dissolving with that one simple question, leaving behind only the tender stirrings of something new, something real.

Her voice trembled with fear, tears welling up in her eyes, and soft sobs escaped her lips.

"**On the 27th of September, 2010, at exactly 8:50 PM,** you came to our house for the first time. Your parents had passed away, and Baba brought you here with him. You entered through the old gate of our previous home—the one that always made a creaking noise. You were wearing a **blue Shalwar kameez**, and the cuff of your right sleeve was rolled up. You were crying when you stepped inside. I was standing on the stairs, watching you... **That was the first time I saw you."**

A faint, bittersweet smile appeared on her face, one that carried both nostalgia and quiet resentment. "And that was the exact moment **I fell in love with you."**

She paused, the smile lingering on her lips, and with a soft, almost sarcastic tone, she whispered:

"You said it so easily... *Do you love me?"*

Zarrar stared at her, lost in her words, captivated by the emotions flowing through her voice.

With a soft, trembling voice, Amira continued, "Whenever we fought as kids, I would always wait, thinking that any moment now, Zarrar will come and make things right. I used to pick fights with you over the smallest things just so you'd come and pacify me... and I could pretend to be upset for a while, only to give in with a bit of drama."

A faint, ironic smile curled on her lips as she shook her head slightly.

"You said it so easily... Do you love me?"

She continued, her voice still trembling with emotion. "I used to finish my homework at school just so I could go watch you play in the evening. I wanted to sit on the sidelines and see you on the field. But you would come to me with that sweet smile and say, **Will you do my homework?** And how could I ever say no?"

Her eyes glistened with unshed tears. "So, I would sit at home with a heavy heart, doing your homework instead. When you returned from your match, Baba would scold you, asking why you made me do your work instead of doing it yourself. And then, you'd get mad at me too."

She paused for a moment, her voice softening with a bittersweet smile. **"But no one ever knew... I wasn't crying because I had to do your work. I cried because doing your homework meant I missed watching you play."**

A faint, ironic smile curled on her lips as she shook her head slightly.

"You said it so easily... Do you love me?"

She continues, "Even seeing you at home all day wasn't enough for me. At school, I would always sit on the front bench, and you on the last. Since you sat on the left side, I would sit on the right, just so every time I turned to talk to my friend, I could catch a glimpse of you behind me."

A faint, ironic smile curled on her lips as she shook her head slightly.

"You said it so easily... Do you love me?"

She continues, "Back then, when you brought snacks, we didn't have much money. But you would buy two snacks for 10 rupees because you loved them so much. You would quickly finish yours, and when I had a little left, I would give it to you, saying, 'Here, you eat it.' God knows how much I loved those snacks too, but you loved them just as much.

My hunger was never truly satisfied, Zarrar—**but seeing you enjoy your favorite snack made me happy.**"

A faint, ironic smile curled on her lips as she shook her head slightly.

"You said it so easily... Do you love me?"

Zarrar listens to her in stunned silence, his hands trembling, guilt gripping him like a vice. It feels as though a storm is raging inside him, and the weight of everything he's done—or failed to do—bears down on him. His heart aches with remorse as he realizes how deeply he has wronged this innocent woman who had only ever loved him selflessly.

Amira softly says, "Wait just two minutes, I'll be right back."

But Zarrar, lost in the gravity of her words, barely registers what she says. She leaves the room briefly, and when she returns, she sits quietly beside him again. Zarrar stares at her, wordlessly, his gaze locked on her as if trying to memorize her face.

Amira holds something behind her back, concealing it, waiting for the right moment to reveal it.

In childhood, there was a time when I fell off my bicycle and hurt my knee, blood oozing out. You took out your handkerchief and pressed it on my wound to stop the bleeding. It was a red handkerchief with black stripes—she reveals the handkerchief she had hidden behind her back, holding it out toward Zarrar.

"This is that handkerchief, Zarrar—I've held onto it for so long, since who knows when. My blood and your sweat are still on it today..."

A faint, ironic smile curled on her lips as she shook her head slightly.

"You said it so easily... 'Do you love me?'" Amira said, looking at Zarrar's face.

Zarrar's fingers gently brushed over the handkerchief, feeling its rough texture as if it were a symbol of the past, and he was silent, his gaze locked on her face.

Every night, I would bring a glass of water to you, knowing very well that I would be the one drinking that water the next day. I came just to have an excuse to be near you, hoping that maybe you would share a bit about your day with me. As I walked away each time, I would glance back, wishing to see if you were watching me, hoping you would stop me for even a little chat...

A faint, ironic smile curled on her lips as she shook her head slightly.

"You said it so easily... Do you love me?"

As she speaks with a quivering voice, her eyes glisten with tears, and her nose is flushed, while damp strands of hair cling to her wet cheeks.

"Zarrar," she begins, her breath hitching, **"I don't know how many years have passed in your love. But God is my witness, I have never looked at anyone in this entire world except you. Every night, I would sleep with the hope that perhaps tomorrow, Zarrar would finally embrace me. But no, you never came."**

Her voice trembles as she continues, **"While the whole world sleeps soundly, I would wake up in the biting cold, pleading with God for you. They say love makes one rebellious, but my love for you has brought me closer to God."**

She takes a deep breath, her chest rising and falling as she gathers her emotions. **"I love you so much that it might take two lifetimes for you to grasp the depth of it. But I've loved not just you, Zarrar, but your very essence, your fragrance."**

Her words hang in the air, heavy with unspoken emotions, as the room seems to fill with a palpable tension, the stillness amplifying the weight of her confession.

Zarrar's tears begin to fall from his eyes as he looks down, his gaze filled with shame. With a trembling voice, he scratches at his palms and whispers, **"Why didn't you ever tell me all this, Amira? Why didn't you say anything..."**

His words hang heavy in the air, a mixture of regret and longing, as he struggles to comprehend the depth of her feelings, feeling the weight of the years lost in silence between them.

Amira smiles through her teary eyes and says, "When your love reaches the point where it must be expressed, understand that for the other person, your declaration of love holds no greater importance than simply satisfying their curiosity Because true love doesn't ask for expression; it is seen on its own. And where were you, really? Always busy in meetings or with Sawera."

Zarrar suddenly looks up, surprised at how Amira knows about Sawera. He feels a wave of embarrassment wash over him, his face reflecting both shame and astonishment.

With a teasing tone, Amira continues, as if she has caught Zarrar in a lie, "Yes, Zarrar — I know about Sawera. It hurt me to think that the time I longed for could so easily be given to someone else. Those eyes — just a glimpse of them meant more to me than all the happiness in the world — were freely available to another."

Tears well up in her eyes as she wipes them away, saying, "Your love was so deeply ingrained in me that no matter how you treated me, I accepted it as my fate and remained content. Yet, every night, I would question myself, '**Am I worthy of this treatment**?' "Then I used to say **that time is like a beautiful moment, a precious gift, given to you. When it comes, you should enjoy it beautifully, but I wasn't even getting that time.**"

"You know," she continues, "**when a person truly loves, they can find a thousand excuses to stay, but if they don't want to stay, they only need one reason to leave.**"

Zarrar gazes at Amira with shameful eyes, words eluding him as if he has been overwhelmed by a debt of kindness he never asked for. He feels lost, unsure of how to express his gratitude for all she has done. Looking up at Amira with teary eyes, he whispers, **"How foolish I have been! I had diamond at home, yet I was searching for it in the market."**

After a brief pause, he takes Amira's hands in his own. She lowers her gaze, unable to meet his eyes. Zarrar continues, "If I had made a mistake, perhaps forgiveness would have come easily. But I have sinned, Amira. I have sinned..."

He moves closer, kneeling at her feet, and breaks down in tears, pleading, "Forgive me, Amira, please forgive me." His head rests in her lap, hands gripping her feet, as he cries out, "Forgive me, Amira, please forgive me..."

This is the same Zarrar who, over the past three years, had never once raised his eyes to look at Amira. Yet today, consumed by love, he has humbled himself at her feet. **In love, there is such power that if someone loves us, we become god, and if we love someone, we become their slaves.**

Amira is taken aback, lost in a whirlwind of emotions, unsure of how to respond to Zarrar's desperation as he clutches her feet in supplication. After a moment, she gently pushes him back, sitting down beside him and tearfully says, "It's strange, this love. No matter how humiliated we feel, just one loving apology can make us crazy in love again."

As she speaks, she embraces him tightly, and they hold each other closely, their tears soaking into one another's shoulders, a poignant reminder of their shared pain and longing.

That night, they talked for hours, as if they were childhood friends reunited after a long separation. They were just the same—laughing and playfully hitting each other as if no time had passed since they last spoke.

Amira glanced at the clock; it was almost 1 AM. "Zarrar, it's getting late. I should head back to my room," she said. Zarrar immediately interjected, "Your room? No way! You're staying here tonight!"

Amira looked at him in surprise, a smile creeping onto her face. "Alright, if that's what you say..."

"Great! From now on, you're sleeping here! This is Your room!" Zarrar exclaimed with enthusiasm.

By 2 AM, they were still lying next to each other, lost in conversation. Amira said softly, "I wish, Zarrar... this moment could last forever."

With a wistful smile, Zarrar replied, **"I wish it could, Amira. Just like this..."**

But as they continued to talk, the warmth of their shared moments enveloped them, and once again, a quiet, melancholic stillness filled the room.

Chapter 6: The Crimson Farewell

It was 4 AM, and the four friends—**Haider**, **Rayan**, **Mani**, and **Hassan**—were deep into their party at a flat in F-6. The music was blasting at full volume, shaking the walls and making the entire place throb with energy. The room was filled with smoke—**weed**, **ice**, and **cigarettes** were in full swing. All four of them were completely intoxicated, lost in their own worlds, while flickering lights and loud sounds added to the chaos.

Haider and Rayan were sprawled on the carpet, laughing uncontrollably, their eyes bloodshot and voices slurred under the weight of intoxication.

Haider takes a puff from his cigarette, a sly grin creeping across his face.

"Bro, Sana thinks I'm taking her seriously. Poor thing's ready to drop everything for me."

Rayan snickers, flicking ash from his joint.

"Same with Saba. She keeps asking, 'Where is this going?' I told her what she wanted to hear, and now she's all in."

Haider chuckles darkly.

"Girls like them? You just tell them what they wanna hear, get what you need, and move on before they catch feelings."

Rayan smirks, exhaling smoke.

"Exactly. Make 'em feel special for a while, and when they ask for more... disappear."

Haider taps his cigarette, grinning.

"Why settle when they're all waiting for a text? Keep 'em on the hook, bro. That's the way."

They exchange a fist bump, laughing smugly as the music thumps louder, drowning the room in beats and smoke.

Meanwhile, Mani sat in the corner, visibly anxious. He kept checking the time on his watch and then glanced nervously at his friends.

"Guys, it's already 4 AM!" Mani exhaled deeply. "I told my parents I'd be back by 9 in the morning. But we haven't even slept yet. How are we supposed to get up in time?" His voice cracked with worry. "If I don't get home by 9, they'll kill me!"

Haider, completely unfazed, leaned back lazily.

"Relax, Mani. Everything will work out. Just enjoy the night, man—no need to stress about it now!"

Hassan was slumped on the sofa in the corner, his eyes shut tight, caught between consciousness and unconsciousness. His head kept lolling from side to side, as though he was trying to grasp what was happening around him, but his mind was long gone. He still held a half-burnt cigarette in his hand, the ash slowly falling onto the floor.

Rayan glanced at Hassan and burst into laughter.

"This guy's gone on a full-blown trip! Think he's ever waking up?"

Mani groaned in frustration, shaking his head.

"Man, just pray we wake up in the morning. Or else, I'm as good as dead!"

23-October-2024

At 5 AM, the alarm rings, shattering the quiet of the room. Zarrar opens his eyes instantly, quickly reaching over to silence it. He sits up, taking a moment to steady his breath, and glances at Amira, who is still fast asleep beside him.

For the first time in years, there's a sense of peace and joy in his heart. *"Never in my life have I experienced a night so beautiful,"* he thinks, a soft smile spreading across his face.

Carefully, he tries to slip out of bed, not wanting to disturb Amira's sleep. But as he moves, his knee bumps into the side table. The glass of water on the table wobbles, almost falling—but Zarrar catches it just in time. The sound, however, is enough to make Amira stir.

She slowly opens her eyes and, upon seeing Zarrar awake, sits up abruptly.

"You're awake?" she asks, rubbing her eyes. "You go do your workout. I'll pray and then make breakfast."

She starts to get up in a hurry, adjusting her shawl, but Zarrar stops her gently.

"Wait—what are you doing?"

Amira gives him a puzzled look.

"Making breakfast..."

A mischievous grin forms on Zarrar's face.

"Not today. Today, I'm making breakfast!"

Amira's eyes widen with disbelief.

"What??"

"Yes, ma'am! I'll make breakfast. You relax for now. Say your prayers in a bit."

Amira chuckles in disbelief.

"But why are *you* making breakfast?"

Zarrar shrugs with a playful smile.

"Because I feel like it!"

Amira sighs, shaking her head.

"Zarrar, this is too much... First, the magic of last night hasn't even worn off, and now you want to make breakfast? Come on, let me do it."

But Zarrar cuts her off firmly.

"I said it. I'll make it."

He moves closer, gently placing his hands on her shoulders and laying her back down on the bed. Covering her with the blanket, he smiles warmly.

"Just sleep now, good girl."

Amira tries to protest through her laughter.

"But Zarrar! How will you even make breakfast?"

Zarrar ignores her protests as he steps out of the room, calling over his shoulder,

"I'm not listening! You just rest."

Amira, now tucked under the blanket, hides her smile. She thinks to herself: *"What's gotten into him all of a sudden?"*

And as the thought lingers, her smile deepens, a warm sense of joy spreading through her. It feels like life has just begun anew.

Zarrar steps out of the bedroom, performing his Fajr prayer first. With his spirit lifted, he heads to the kitchen, pondering over what to make for breakfast. After a moment's thought, he decides that an omelet with paratha would be perfect.

Unbeknownst to anyone, Zarrar is a surprisingly good cook. He quickly gets to work, whipping up a breakfast fit for two. As soon as an idea comes to his mind, he gets excited: *"My car accident is at 5 o'clock, and if we go for lunch at 2, she'll be happy too. If Amira and I go out for lunch at a nice place today, she would be so delighted. And, maybe in this way, I can also ease the anxiety from my dream."*

After setting the breakfast table, he heads to the bedroom door, knocking gently.

"Madam, breakfast is ready. Come on out!"

From inside, Amira's voice echoes back:

"Zarrar, I'm not coming. You go ahead and have breakfast."

Zarrar, not catching her words clearly, laughs and says,

"Alright, great."

Then, suddenly startled, he stops:

"Wait, what? What did you just say, Amira?"

She hesitates, her tone shy:

"Zarrar... I can't."

Confused, Zarrar asks:

"What do you mean, 'can't'?"

There's a brief silence before Amira chuckles softly:

"I feel... shy."

Zarrar laughs, placing his hand on his forehead:

"Amira, are you kidding me?"

"No, Zarrar... I just can't."

With a playful grin, Zarrar replies:

"Alright, Amira. If you don't come out, I'll come in, grab your hand, and bring you out myself. And then you'll feel *really* shy!"

Amira quickly interrupts:

"No, no! Don't come in—I'm coming out!"

Zarrar nods with a smile, satisfied:

"Good. Now, be at the table in two minutes!"

Zarrar sits at the table, smiling softly as he waits. Just then, Amira shyly steps out of the room, her eyes widening in surprise as she sees the beautifully arranged breakfast on the table. She sits across from Zarrar, her curiosity apparent.

"Did you make all of this yourself?" she asks, awe in her voice.

Zarrar chuckles, his smile widening. "What did you think? I can do everything."

Amira takes in the spread before her, drawn in by its aroma. "It all looks so delicious," she says, her eyes sparkling.

Zarrar leans in and says, "Now you should put this on Snap or Insta Story."

She looks at him with a hint of amusement. "I don't have Instagram or Snapchat," she replies casually.

A flicker of surprise crosses Zarrar's face. "Why not?"

Amira glances down, a slight blush coloring her cheeks. **"You once said that you didn't like Instagram or Snapchat, remember?"**

Zarrar looks at her, a warm smile spreading across his face. "What kind of a person are you, Amira?"

Amira laughs lightly and replies, "Whoever I am, however I am, I am yours. "

They both start eating breakfast, and Amira takes the first bite, showering him with praise, pausing every so often to compliment him again, clearly delighted with each bite.

Zarrar says, "Alright, Amira, let's have dinner together tonight, around 2. Come with the driver on time, and I'll meet you there." Amira softly asks, "Will you be free?"

"Yes, that's why I'm saying let's have a nice dinner," Zarrar replies.

With a smile, Amira asks, "But which restaurant, Zarrar?"

Thinking for a moment, he says, "Skylight Café by Roomy."

Amira's face lights up with excitement. "That sounds amazing!" she exclaims.

Just then, Zarrar stands up, saying, "I'll need to head out now; I have some work to take care of."

Amira nods, "Yes, yes, please go ahead."

With a smile, Zarrar adds, "Take your time and enjoy your breakfast, madam." And with that, he heads out to get ready for his day.

Zarrar gets ready, wearing the same suit he's been wearing for days, giving it a quick brush to freshen it up. He slips his watch onto his wrist, only to realize it's stopped. "It's... stopped," he murmurs to himself, a flicker of surprise on his face.

Just then, Amira appears in the doorway, holding his phone. "I charged it for you," she says with a light smile. "And please, reply when I message you, alright?" Zarrar chuckles, "Alright, promise."

As he heads towards the door, Amira calls after him, "Zarrar..." He turns instantly, "Yes, Amira?"

For a moment, she hesitates, her eyes sparkling as if she wants to say something significant, but instead, she simply says, "Oh, never mind... I'll tell you later today, Zarrar." There's a faint smile on her lips, and Zarrar, catching her expression, shyly lowers his gaze, "Of course, Amira, of course."

They stand in silence, eyes filled with emotions left unspoken. Then, Zarrar finally opens the door and steps outside. Just before getting into his car, he turns, lifting a hand to wave goodbye.

Amira, standing in the doorway, beams back, waving him off enthusiastically. Zarrar gets into the car and drives away, disappearing down the road.

The morning was beautiful; the sun and clouds danced across the sky, casting shadows that came and went. Zarrar parked his car by the side of the road and started walking down the familiar path he had been taking for the past few days. This path led him to a quietness that brought peace to his heart, as he visited the elder regularly.

When he reached the elder's house, he saw a crowd gathered outside. Confused, he asked a man nearby, "Brother, what's going on here?"

The man replied softly, "The Old Man... he has passed away."

Zarrar's feet felt glued to the ground as the weight of the words sank in. Memories of his conversations with the elder filled his mind. For a moment, he just stood there, his head bowed in sorrow, watching as people brought the elder's body outside for the funeral procession.

He joined silently, walking behind the mourners. They reached the cemetery, where the elder's sons began the burial. Zarrar stood off to the side, his heart heavy with grief as he recalled the elder's words of wisdom. When the burial was complete and people began to disperse, Zarrar approached the grave.

With tears streaming down his face and a faint smile, he whispered, "You liked my 'I love you' so much that you accepted it as my last words to you." His voice cracked, and the tears he had held back finally flowed freely, his heart overcome with love and sorrow.

A little distance away, a man noticed Zarrar crying and motioned to his companion. They walked over, one of them greeting him, "Assalamu Alaikum!"

Zarrar lifted his head to see them.

"Who are you... to our father?" one of them asked gently.

Zarrar wiped his tears and quietly asked, "What was your father's name?"

The two brothers looked at each other, puzzled, then back at him. "Our father's name was **Muzaffar Hussain Khan,**" one replied. "But if you didn't even know his name, why are you crying here like this?"

Zarrar's eyes glistened with tears, but a calm serenity graced his face. Smiling softly, he said, "You wouldn't understand God's wisdom, brothers. You stayed with them for over 30 years and learned nothing, while I stayed with them for just 2 days and learned what I couldn't learn in 20 years. "

Then, reaching into his coat pocket, he pulled out an envelope, handing it to one of the brothers. "This is the debt your father owed. Please, pay it off to those he was indebted to."

As he turned to leave, he looked back, saying, "God never forgets how we treat His creation. Remember, He will remind you through your own sons, of the hardships you put your father through."

With that, Zarrar walked away. The brothers called out to him, but without looking back, he continued on his path, fading into the distance.

As Zarrar walked back, he spotted the two benches he and the elder used to sit on. Wiping his tears, he murmured, **"Maybe this is the last time I'll sit here."** He approached the bench slowly, as if he wanted to seal this moment in his heart forever.

October's chill swept through the air. Crimson, brittle leaves scattered with the breeze, like memories drifting away into the past. The sky was bright, yet the sun was hidden behind clouds, faintly reminding of its presence, like silent tears hidden behind a smile. The whole scene held the weight of a goodbye, as if nature itself was preparing for one final, silent farewell.

There were distant sounds of children's laughter and the rustling of dried leaves underfoot, mingled with the soft chirping of birds resting on barren branches. Every sound seemed tinged with nostalgia, a quiet sadness for something lost. This atmosphere, the gentle wind, the silence—it all seemed to remind him how much beauty one overlooks, lost in the purposeless anxieties of life.

In the calm, cold atmosphere, lost in his thoughts, Zarrar finds himself talking to himself. He asks questions and answers them as if comforting his own heart. "How can we humans ever truly understand God's wisdom? I was wandering aimlessly down this path when suddenly I met the elder. Through him, Allah guided me, helped me find a direction, and even resolved his life's issue through me before calling him back to Himself. Isn't it beautiful? Sometimes Allah brings us to others just for our good or theirs."

He takes a deep breath, watching the fallen leaves as if making room for new ones. It's a reminder, he thinks, of life's lessons. "These temporary victories and losses—they mean nothing. The real defeat is only when we accept it in our hearts. Otherwise, what's the point of winning or losing? Did the winner truly gain anything meaningful, or did the loser truly lose something? These are just illusions we create for ourselves."

He continues, speaking softly to the silence around him. "We're the ones who assign value to things. Tear up a plain paper, and it's nothing. But tear a currency note, and suddenly, it's a big deal. Tears shed in joy are fine, but in sadness, they carry a weight. A stone is meaningless, but carve it into a statue, and people start worshiping it. If a friend says something casually, we laugh it off, but the same thing from a stranger can sting. All of it is a trick of perception, principles we ourselves have created and gotten tangled up in."

Suddenly, his thoughts are interrupted by the ping of a message. He pulls out his phone, glancing at the screen, and a faint smile crosses his lips. It's a message from Sawera, saying, "Zarrar, please forgive me. It's not what you think." With a bitter smile, he replies, **"Your absence has beautifully altered my state; now, every word you once said feels like a lie."** He sends the message, blocks her, and puts his phone away. Lost once more in his thoughts, he seems to have decided to close this chapter of his life for good.

Lost in his thoughts, Zarrar was talking to himself, "How strange I was, content with so little love. Just a few sweet words from her had me captivated, but perhaps that was my biggest mistake. **People say that eyes never lie, but do they really always tell the truth?** Isn't the best actor in films the one who can use his eyes to express everything? So why wouldn't eyes lie? **Or maybe her eyes weren't lying, and I just saw what I wanted to see.**

The truth is that divinity exists among us humans; respect has become so rare in our time that when we give it to someone, along with love, that person feels like they are GOD. But how can a human truly be a GOD? Often, the very person who receives love from us ends up pushing us toward resentment. One thing is certain: a person who cannot respect you can never truly love you. If respect doesn't exist between two people, their relationship cannot last for long. I believe people are inherently good—very good. The problem is that we ask for respect and love from people who have no intention of giving it, and this is the root of our downfall. Everyone is out there begging for scraps of dignity, but people forget that they themselves are worthy of respect. Begging is something they've chosen for themselves, but they're deserving of much more. Humans are incredibly beautiful beings. Try loving them, and you'll see; they're so beautiful that a single compliment can make them remember you for a lifetime.

Everything that is beautiful in this world and everything that truly benefits us comes to us without a price. The most breathtaking view — the rising and setting of the sun — is freely given, asking nothing in return. A mother's love, the deepest and purest of all, comes to us unconditionally. The comfort of lying in our own bed, the tranquility felt when watching a tree gracefully shed its leaves — these blessings are ours, without effort or cost.

Our friends, the ones who became part of our lives so naturally, offer a comfort and peace unmatched by anything else. And the love given freely by someone, knowing fully that we may never return it, is one of the most beautiful things in the world. The beating of my heart, the way the clouds absorb and release rain into the earth — all of this is free.

There is beauty in this realization, but also a bittersweet truth. Beauty, because how simple it is to enjoy these gifts. And sadness, because the things given to us for free, we often fail to truly value.

He was lost in his thoughts when suddenly a voice called out, "Shani! It's going to be great! Shani's going to have fun!" A man hopped and skipped his way over, stopping right in front of Zarrar with an excited grin and said, "Mom's making parathas; it's going to be amazing! Shani's happy, Shani's so happy!" Zarrar smiled, as if he finally understood Shani, and softly said, **"Eat to your heart's content, Shani!"** Shani, hearing this, bounced away, happily shouting with joy.

Lost in thought, Zarrar felt as if life itself had paused in a quiet circle. Speaking to himself, he murmured, "True life, it's Shani who's truly living it, free from every sorrow. Perhaps humanity's greatest burden is wondering what people will think, and here is someone utterly free from it all. To him, a paratha made by his mother is the greatest wealth."

He stopped briefly, reflecting, "We're slaves of our own making, fearing people's opinions more than death itself. We live not for our happiness but to please others. Who knows when we'll finally realize that the peace we seek is hidden in a secluded, wooden cabin in a silent forest. That unique comfort found in a barren forest cabin can't be found in a bustling city. The peace hidden in fallen red leaves can't be found in a Red rose. Humanity has become caught up in a race, and the more material things surround us, the hollower we become inside."

Zarrar's thoughts turned even deeper, "This progress may make us look beautiful on the outside, but it's also making our existence reek. Today, those who once faced wars are now helpless in front of Instagram's algorithm. No wonder those rich people, who possess every luxury in the world, stand at the brink of divorce. Meanwhile, those who struggle for a meal live in peace. Complaints of betrayal and unfaithfulness come from the rich people or free people or may be from those who are living a good life, while the poor man eats his simple meal and rests."

Then, Zarrar jolted, "What am I saying? Have I suddenly become a philosopher? Where are these thoughts coming from? What's happening to me?" And his mind shifted to a new train of thought, "The most beautiful moments of our lives, they're our childhood, where words had no other meaning, where the future didn't even matter."

He pondered further, "The beauty of childhood lies in that simplicity, and the real sorrow is that it slips away without warning. Ah, what an injustice — such a bitter tragedy. The day we skip watching cartoons before heading to school, that's the day childhood ends. When, one evening, we return from playing outside and never go back out again, that's the day our childhood is over. The day we no longer watch that movie we used to see again and again, childhood ends. When a favorite singer or actor from childhood passes away, that day also marks the end of childhood. And when those cousins who shared our childhood start getting married, it's another goodbye. When we leave the house where we spent those childhood days, it's the last day of that era. And when those elders who once rushed us to the hospital for every little bruise now struggle to walk themselves, only then do we realize that childhood has truly slipped away."It's a strange phenomenon; as the moment nears, there's happiness, but once it's over, a sense of sadness settles in. **"I don't want to die—oh God, I don't want to die."** Isn't it ironic that when a person finally learns the art of living, when life starts to feel fulfilling, that's when death approaches? Why couldn't I learn anything from my own life? Life and history walk hand in hand. Our lives are just a collection of stories that repeat in the same way every time, as if it's happening for the first time. Only the faces change, the times shift, but the characters and the stories remain the same. And it's wonderful how God keeps repeating this history until we finally learn from it.

His mind was lost in thoughts, sometimes one, sometimes another. In one moment, he thought, the more the pain and suffering, the bigger the rosary in his hand becomes. Then in the next, he thought, betrayal and treachery—these are the two things that either make a person a hero or a villain, but they completely transform a person. Suddenly, another thought struck his mind, ***"Beauty will destroy this world."*** The lives of the ugly are ruined by the beautiful faces. The beauty of AI will destroy the human race. The beauty of a rainstorm sweeps away someone's home, and a beautiful house or car becomes the target of a thief's nightly deeds. Someone's beautiful clothes become a mockery for someone else who wears simple clothes. And this beauty is nothing but a facade, a deception that hides the truth of a person, never revealing their true essence. The glossy mask of beauty hides the inner ugliness and outdated thoughts, which fade away with time. Those who drown in the superficial beauty of this world are often unaware of the depth of their own soul, and in this deception, they stray far from their true selves.

His thoughts had no stoppage. He was asking himself questions and answering them at the same time.

At that moment, Zarrar's phone chimes again. This time, it's a message from Amira. She's sent him a picture, half-ready, with a caption that reads, "For you—your Amira is getting ready. Don't be late, just come quickly... there's so much to talk about." Zarrar smiles for a moment and replies, "I'm on my way, can't wait to see you, just." Then he says to himself, "Come on, Zarrar, life is so beautiful. Learn from these red leaves; only when they fall and scatter after their time has passed does their beauty truly emerge. Meaningless are the deaths of those without a story, with no one to remember them. Get up, Zarrar—someone's waiting for you, and even God doesn't keep loved ones waiting."

Zarrar rises from the bench, takes a deep breath, and says, **"If there is life, let it be like this."** With these words, he starts to walk, leaving behind a trail of falling leaves. The sky grows completely dark, as if wrapped in shadows. The rain is on the brink of pouring, while the heavens rumble with thunder and flashes of lightning.

Amira stands in front of the mirror, getting ready. As she's putting on her earrings, her phone lights up with a message notification. Her fingers, with a slight tremble of excitement, reach for the phone. Seeing Zarrar's name, her eyes light up, and a gentle blush colors her cheeks as she reads his message. Holding the phone close to her chest, she takes a deep breath and whispers to herself, "If only this evening would never end, if only this season—this day—could linger forever."

Zarrar is deeply engrossed, busy organizing a meal for nearly two hundred underprivileged people, seated together on a large spread. He's arranging the food on the tablecloth, giving instructions to his team on how to serve. The faces of these two hundred hungry souls light up with joy and disbelief, experiencing a feast beyond their imagination. They savor biryani and roast chicken – a banquet they could only dream of. In a booming voice, Zarrar calls out, "Eat to your heart's content, and on your way back, take some rice home for your families."

Stepping back, Zarrar watches them eat from a short distance, lost in thought. A memory flashes, and he quickly pulls out his phone, dialing his secretary Anum. Even while speaking on the call, his gaze remains fixed on the people, who look back at him with wonder and gratitude. They wonder, is this a human, or an angel, someone who not only feeds them but gives them dignity and warmth.

Zarrar: "Salaam, Anum!"

Anum: "Wa Alaikum Salaam, Sir!"

Zarrar (filled with joy and excitement): "Anum, I don't have words to thank you enough. Managing everything for 200 people in such a short time is no small feat, and you handled it all so well. I'll always be grateful."

Anum (falls silent for a moment, then replies): "Sir, what are you saying? You requested it, and I couldn't have said no. It was no trouble."

Zarrar (gently, with a hint of remorse): "Anum, I'm truly thankful to you. But I also owe you an apology." (pauses for a few seconds) "Over these past few years, I've put you through a lot, and I regret that. I apologize for it all."

Anum (momentarily silent, surprised, lost in thought): "No, sir, it's really nothing. There's no issue."

Zarrar: "Still, I'd feel better if you'd forgive me."

Anum (quickly responds): "No, sir, there's no need. You're our boss; you have that right."

Zarrar (smiling softly): "It seems God has decided to reward your patience. Your salary is being raised by 25%. Now you'll be able to work even more joyfully."

Anum (laughing in happiness, almost in disbelief): "Thank you, sir. I can't believe it."

Zarrar (laughing): "Try to believe it, and let me just check on things here."

Anum (excitedly): "Yes, sir, thank you so much!"

Zarrar ends the call with a satisfied smile, and his face radiates contentment as he happily watches the scene unfolding before him.

Zarrar is in his car, heading toward his destination, while Amira, too, is on her way to the restaurant.

Meanwhile, Haider, Rayan, Mani, and Hassan are all packed into another car, speeding down the road. Having been up all night and slightly intoxicated, the four friends race forward.

Mani (worriedly): "Guys, we're super late. The folks are gonna be mad. But Haider, slow down, man! This isn't a racetrack!"

Hassan: "Haider, seriously, you're going way too fast. Slow it down, bro. You're gonna get us in trouble."

Haider (excitedly, responding): "What do you both want from me? I'm dropping Mani home, right? What else could you want? Rayan, make them understand."

Rayan: "What, have we kept little girls with us? Man up, boys! Nothing's gonna happen. Chill, just chill."

Mani (angrily): "That's it; I'm done coming along with you guys. You take everything as a joke!"

Hassan (softly, trying to calm him): "Just ignore it, Mani. They'll never get it."

Haider (laughing, teasing): "Look at these two delicate little princesses of mine!"

Haider drifts sharply around a corner, sending the car spinning. He and Rayan burst into laughter.

Rayan: "Live a little, my friends! Enjoy life!"

Mani sits quietly, fuming, while Hassan looks on with concern, noticing his friend's growing frustration.

Driving along the road, Zarrar spots the famous Flower Market in F7, where a vibrant flower shop catches his eye. He pulls his car up right in front of the shop and is about to step out when he pauses and starts laughing to himself. "Remember the last time I bought flowers?" he says with a grin.

He then goes to start the car again, chuckling, "If I hadn't taken my time with those flowers that day, I wouldn't have heard those words at the right moment. Flowers—they're innocent, really. It's people who either treasure them in books or toss them aside."

With that, he turns off the car once more, steps out, and picks out a bouquet of beautiful roses. Taking a small card as well, Zarrar sits back in his car, reaches for a pen, and writes something heartfelt on the card. A smile lights up his face as he attaches the note to the bouquet, satisfied with this quiet, meaningful gesture.

It was exactly 2:17 PM. Heavy clouds had cast a gloomy silence across the sky, colliding with each other and echoing ominous sounds, almost like cries of despair. A cold wind swept through, bringing with it the chill of winter's first rain. It felt as if the sky's heart was weighed down with sorrow, ready to break at any moment and release torrents of tears, flooding the earth with its grief.

Zarrar reached the restaurant and parked his car along the road. Just then, a sudden downpour began, with fierce gusts of wind. Sitting in his car, he watched as the rain lashed against his windshield, his gaze fixed on the sorrow-laden clouds above. For a moment, he felt the weight of something unspoken within him, as if sharing in the sky's melancholy. As the rain grew heavier, Zarrar decided to wait a little longer, as if this quiet patience held a meaning deeper than words.

Mani (voice trembling with worry): Haider, please slow down, man. The rain is pouring so hard, slow down, please, before something happens.

Hassan (seriously): Mani's right. It's rush hour, man. Haider, just ease up a bit.

Rayan (carelessly): You two sound like you've lost it! Enjoy this weather; moments like this don't come back!

Haider, taking Rayan's words to heart, turns up the music and says, "I just want silence now, nothing else." With that, he presses the accelerator, pushing the car even faster, overtaking the passing car in a way that could easily lead to disaster. Rain beats against the windshield as though the world itself braced for an impending tragedy.

Hassan and Mani shout out, "Are you crazy, Haider?" Even Rayan, shocked, says, "Haider, what are you doing, man? This almost turned into an accident!"

Haider, anger flashing in his eyes as he turns the car sharply, snaps, "Next time, I'm not coming with you guys. You're all like kids—scared of everything. Now, watch what I'm going to do!" He pushes the car faster, as if daring fate, testing his own and everyone's limits.

Zarrar is sitting in his car when Amira's call comes in. He quickly picks up the phone and answers.

Amira: "Zarrar, where are you?"

Zarrar: "I've arrived; I'm just coming."

Amira: "Hurry, Zarrar! The rain is really heavy, and I'm getting scared."

Zarrar smiles, a glint of warmth in his eyes. "Why are you afraid? I'm here."

Amira: "I'm already here; where are you?"

Zarrar: "If you've arrived, then I'm just a moment away." He opens the car door, steps out, and takes the flowers with him. The rain pours down harder, drenching him instantly. The wind is fierce, making his clothes and the flowers sway in the air.

Amira: "Where are you, Zarrar?"

Zarrar steps out and looks around, spotting Amira seated inside through the glass window. He smiles, a bit shyly, and says, **"I'm right in front of you, madam! Just take a look."**

Haider laughs, saying, "Watch this, kids. That guy standing over there? I'll scare him so bad, but it'll be you guys who end up screaming!" He speeds up, getting dangerously close to Zarrar, as if he'll crash any second.

Inside the car, all three voices plead, "Haider, don't do it! Please, that's enough!"

Meanwhile, Amira blushes, smiling as she sees Zarrar across the street. Standing in the pouring rain, his coat billowing in the fierce wind, he lifts his phone and waves with a soft smile.

Suddenly, Zarrar glances to his left, and his heart sinks as he sees a car veering uncontrollably toward him. There's no time to think; it's as if, for a moment, he's already left this world. He lowers his hand and catches sight of his watch, realizing that the death he thought would come at **5 p.m. was arriving now, at 2 p.m.—the watch had shown the wrong time all along.**

There's barely a moment left. He glances at Amira one last time, and a gentle smile crosses his face, as though he understands it's his final one.

Haider brings the car even closer, but due to water on the road, it skids uncontrollably and slams into Zarrar. Zarrar's body, along with the bouquet he held, flies over the hood and lands on the ground as the car crashes into a tree, bringing it down as well. The bouquet lies scattered on the wet road, its petals crushed, trampled by the passing cars as they drive through the rain, unaware of the tragedy that has just unfolded.

Amira witnesses the entire scene. Her phone falls from her hand, and she collapses onto her chair in shock. Zarrar's face is drenched in blood, his lifeless body lying in the rain as the water begins to wash the blood from his face. One of his eyes remains open, and through the blurred haze, he sees people rushing toward him. He takes a deep breath, with the hint of a smile on his face, and attempts another—but this breath never escapes.

Someone rushes to him, supporting his head and turning him slightly. One side of his face is clear, the other stained with blood, and from his open eye, a lone tear falls to the ground as he smiles for the last time and his breath fades away. Zarrar's life ends there.

A crowd quickly gathers, and a thunderous cloud echoes across the sky, as if the heavens themselves mourn the passing of Zarrar Shah. He has bid farewell to this world forever. **A crimson leaf floats in the rainwater, drifting until it finally comes to rest against Zarrar's still body. Like the leaf, Zarrar too has been gently severed from this world—departing quietly yet eternally, leaving behind a beauty and depth that will be remembered.**

www.ingramcontent.com/pod-product-compliance
Lightning Source LLC
LaVergne TN
LVHW010455160826
845677LV00012B/2499

* 9 7 9 8 2 3 0 6 6 1 7 4 0 *